PROTECTING
Piper

New York Times & USA Today Bestselling Author
CYNTHIA EDEN

This book is a work of fiction. Any similarities to real people, places, or events are not intentional and are purely the result of coincidence. The characters, places, and events in this story are fictional.

Published by Hocus Pocus Publishing, Inc.

Copyright ©2019 by Cindy Roussos

All rights reserved. This publication may not be reproduced, distributed, or transmitted in any form without the express written consent of the author except for the use of small quotes or excerpts used in book reviews.

Copy-editing by: J. R. T. Editing

CHAPTER ONE

"Okay, you're going to be pissed, but you need help."

Piper Lane glanced up from her spot on the floor. She'd been meticulously cleaning the wreckage left in her home. The cops had finally given her the all clear to go back inside and actually touch things again, and she'd just wanted to get the place back in shape.

But at her best friend's words, a cold knot formed in her stomach. "The cops *are* helping me, Ben. They searched for prints, they collected evidence, and they're even going to send some patrols around the neighborhood to keep an eye on things."

Ben's handsome face tensed. "You need more help than that, and you know it. This is the *second* time you've been targeted. This isn't just some break-in bullshit. And if you'd come to me the *first* time this happened—"

She rose to her feet. "I don't come running to you every time something bad happens in my life."

His blue eyes widened. "Why the hell not? That's what *best friends* are for! I watch your sexy ass and you watch mine!"

Okay, granted, Ben did have a sexy ass. The scrawny kid she'd known as a child had turned into a drop-dead gorgeous guy. They'd been each other's shadows ever since they'd met in Pre-K. He'd been trying to eat glue, and she'd shown him the error of his ways. Since that moment, they'd been inseparable all through school. Ben knew most of her secrets, he could tell when she was lying, and generally, he was her rock.

She hadn't gone to him with this particular problem, though, because...

A knock sounded at her door.

Piper squeezed her eyes shut. "For the love of God and pugs, please tell me that isn't who I think it is."

Ben sighed, a long and not-sorry sound. "I had to call him. It's his *thing*."

Her eyes cracked open in time to see Ben turn away and stride toward the front door. Every muscle in her body locked down when he curled his fingers around the doorknob. The last forty-eight hours had been hell for Piper. She'd gotten back in town to find her home absolutely trashed. The cops had told her to stay out of the place while they conducted their investigation, so she'd been moved to a local motel with just the clothes on her back. Then she'd been told that the cops had pretty much turned up nothing.

And now…now *this*.

Now…him.

She rushed across the room. "Calling him was a mistake—"

Too late. She'd collided with Ben's broad back, and he'd just opened the door. And her nemesis filled the doorway.

Eric freaking Wilde. All six-foot-three inches of trouble. Even taller than Ben, even wider in the shoulders, and, damn him…even sexier. *Not* that she would have ever told Eric that fact. The guy was smug enough as it was.

He wore tailored slacks, a white button-down, and a black tie that hung loosely around his neck. A stylish, black coat clung to his powerful shoulders. His eyes—not blue like Ben's but a dark, dark brown—immediately found her as she stood there, gaping at him. No, correction, glaring. A faint smile curved his lips as he held her stare. A smile, that, if anything, looked like a smirk on his sensual mouth.

"What's the big emergency?" Eric demanded. His eyes narrowed on her as she clutched Ben's arm. "What was such a big deal that I had to rush right over with no explanation?"

Eric hadn't seen the rest of her place. Actually, he probably hadn't seen *any* of it. She and Ben were blocking the entrance. Maybe there was still time to get Eric out of her home before it was too late. "Uh…" Piper began as her hand dropped down and clutched tightly to Ben's.

Eric's gaze fell to their now joined hands. His jaw hardened. "You two finally making things official?" His already deep voice turned into a growl. "That what this is about? You wanted me to come over so you could tell me in person that you're getting married?"

Getting *what*? Piper looked at Ben. Ben looked at Piper. And then her best friend in the entire world said—

"Hell, no!"

Piper felt her cheeks burn. *Way to be subtle.*

Ben shook his head. "Piper has a problem, bro. One that is scaring the hell out of me." Ben's voice was dead serious. He used his hold on Piper's hand to pull her from the doorway. "Take a look for yourself."

Eric's hard gaze slid around her den. "What the fuck?" He stepped into the house, moving out of the doorway, and he slammed the door shut behind him.

She winced at the loud bang.

"Who did this?" Eric demanded. She knew his burning stare had taken in everything. The slashed couch cushions. The shattered picture frames. The broken vases. The smashed TV.

"If we knew," Ben fired right back, "then I wouldn't have called you!"

Piper wrapped her arms around her stomach. "This is a breaking and entering case. The cops said things like this—unfortunately—happen too often in Atlanta." Her voice came out nice and steady, a good sign. She needed to appear in control. "This isn't the type of case that you handle, Eric. You're into corporate security and celebrity protection bits." *The rich and famous.* "Ben didn't need to call you. It's nothing."

But Eric stalked toward her with his slow, lethal grace. He moved silently. He always did. She'd never quite figured out how a man so big could move without making a whisper of sound.

He stopped right in front of her. She tipped back her head so that she could meet his dark stare.

"Someone broke into your home. Someone destroyed your things." A muscle jerked along his rock-hard jaw. A jaw that was covered with just the faintest of five o'clock shadows. "That isn't nothing. It's something very big to me."

"And to me!" Ben piped up. "That's why I had to call you. The cops did their routine, but they turned up nothing, and seeing as how this is the second time that—"

Eric held up one hand. "Second time?" His gaze never left Piper's face.

"Uh, yeah." Ben cleared his throat. "This is the second time someone has broken into her place. The first time was about a month ago, when she was out of town on another business trip. The place wasn't destroyed, though, and the cops barely glanced anywhere then." Now he shot Piper his disapproving frown. "Not that I knew about that incident at the time, since Piper has apparently decided to start keeping secrets from her *best* friend."

Seriously? "It wasn't a secret. You were busy back then." A big case at his firm. "And I didn't think it was a big deal. I handled it."

"*Handled* it?" Eric's voice was low and lethal.

He'd always done that. Gotten quiet when he was at his most dangerous. Other people yelled. Their faces turned red. Not Eric. Oh, sure, he was angry, she could see the fury hardening his gaze. And that quiet, gravelly voice…*Crap, he's pissed.*

Piper squared her shoulders. "You didn't need to come here," she whispered.

"I should have been here a *month* ago," he rasped right back. "What did the bastard do when he broke in then?"

She shivered. "It was…a few things were just re-arranged. Some photos. Some stuff in my bedroom." And she was flushing again. Jeez. When she'd called the cops about that break-in, they'd looked at her as if she was crazy. The uniforms had suggested that maybe she'd been the one to rearrange things and that Piper had just forgotten that she'd moved the items.

They'd blown her off.

When they'd seen all the destruction left in her home this time, though, their response had been different.

"What stuff in your bedroom?" Eric's gaze held her in place.

She swallowed and cast an anxious glance Ben's way. Ben. The traitor. He *knew* she hadn't wanted to involve Eric. Didn't she go out of her way to avoid Ben's too-fierce older brother? The guy made her nervous. Edgy. Always had.

"Piper…"

The way Eric said her name sent a shiver over her. And she didn't even know if it was the good or bad kind of shiver.

"Don't look at Ben," Eric told her, voice rumbling. "Look at me. Talk to *me*."

Huffing out a breath, she brought her gaze back to him. "My underwear, okay? It was moved around. So was the stuff in my nightgown drawer. I swear, someone was in my bedroom, and it creeped me out. But the cops couldn't find any evidence back then."

"They didn't find jack this time, either," Ben muttered. "Said the place was wiped down."

"This isn't your kind of job," she told Eric as her spine remained perfectly straight. "There was no need for Ben to bother you about this. I'm sorry you came here and wasted your time."

Eric gave a slow shake of his dark head. His thick hair slid back from his forehead. "This is my job. And you are never a bother or a waste of time to me."

What? "Since when?" The words just kind of blurted out of her, but her normal self-control was gone. It had been blasted away by the stress of the last forty-eight hours. To know that someone had come into her home *again*. That someone had destroyed all of her belongings. She felt violated and angry and scared, and she was trying hard to hold herself together. But…bam. Now Eric was here.

And her self-control had never been at its best when he was around.

No one could make her angrier than Eric.

No one could make her feel more vulnerable.

And…deep, dark secret…no one had ever made her *want* more than him.

But the desire did not go both ways. He barely tolerated her most days, and on the other days, Eric just stayed the hell away from her. It was how their relationship worked. Or, didn't work.

"I'll find him. I'll figure out who did this. You don't have to worry." Eric gave a determined nod.

Her jaw pretty much hit the floor. "I can't afford you!" A hard truth. "I just started my business a few months ago. The gallery is up and barely running, and I've put all of my money into it. I-I know how much you charge your clients, and I just can't pay—"

"Fuck the payment. I'm doing this for you." His eyes glittered.

Once more, her gaze shot to Ben.

"Why do you do that?" Eric's voice had dropped even more. Turned into a low whisper that she didn't think Ben could hear. Eric had closed in on her, moving so silently. "Why always look to him even when I'm standing right in front of you?"

Her heart seemed to jerk in her chest. Just that fast—her stare whipped back to him. This time, she didn't look away. She couldn't. And the way he was staring at her…

So much intensity. So much heat.

Eric's hand lifted and touched her cheek. "You're coming home with me."

Ben made a choking sound. "Whoa! Hold up." And, in a flash, he was there, grabbing Eric's arm and pulling him away from Piper. "Look, we all know how you can shift into overprotective mode. Especially where Piper is concerned."

Especially where Piper is concerned. Um, since when? And *she* certainly didn't know that interesting little tidbit about Eric. She generally thought he just shifted into annoyed mode.

"But slow your roll." Ben flashed his killer smile. The one that showcased his matching dimples. Eric didn't have dimples. He had a hard slash in his right cheek. One that came out on the very rare occasions when he gave a full, mouth-stretching smile. "We all need to take a breath, okay?"'

Piper sucked in about four breaths.

"Eric, I called you because I wanted your expertise. Piper obviously needs a new security system installed at this place. I thought you could help. Thought you could point us in the right direction." Ben shrugged. "I didn't call you here so that you could carry Piper away!" He gave a laugh.

Eric was still staring at her, and he wasn't laughing. "That's exactly what I'm going to do. Time's up, *bro*."

"I think I'm lost," Piper muttered. Her temples were throbbing. She lifted a hand and rubbed at her right temple. "Look, it's been a long day. Long week. Long month. I appreciate you coming over, Eric, and, yes, I do need some advice on a new security system." Advice would be great. Fabulous.

"I'll get a member of my team to install an upgraded system immediately. Until then, grab a bag because you're coming with me."

That was the thing with Eric. The guy could be so incredibly bossy. Yes, he ran a huge company. And, yes, he *was* the boss man there. But right then...Piper just sighed. "I know the word *please* has to be in your vocabulary, somewhere. I mean, I've met your parents. They're great people, and I know they taught you manners." She pointed to Ben. "He says please. And thank you. And he acts courteous and gentlemanly, and—"

A low growl came from Eric. "Ben's the charmer. We all know that shit." Eric took a step toward her. A ripple of muscle. A glide of sensual movement. Why did she always notice that stuff about him? Voice rumbling, he continued grimly,

"But you don't need charm right now. You need someone who can kick ass. That's what I do. I eliminate threats. I make problems go away. *You* have a problem, so I will make it vanish."

"Out of the goodness of your heart?" Her head tilted. No, she wasn't buying that bit. Any goodness Eric had inside had never been directed at her.

"I'll do it because you're in danger, and you know it."

Her body iced. She did know it.

"You're trying to bluff and act like you're tough, but you're scared. Ben knows it, he can see past your lie. That's why he called me. *I* can see past the lie, too. You look at what this SOB did to your place, you look at the rage, and you're afraid."

Yes, she was. And she was trying to act tough, but so what? A woman had to keep her shit together in this world.

"The fact that someone was here before, that someone fucking messed with your underwear…" Eric's hands clenched and unclenched at his sides. "I've seen situations like this get bad, fast."

She cleared her throat. "The cops said there was no way to know if it was the same intruder—"

Eric just gave a hard shake of his head. "If you've got a stalker, if you've got some jerk who's obsessed with you, he's accelerating.

Accelerating leads to bolder acts. And it can lead to *physical* attacks."

Something she already feared. Was this the time to tell him that there had been a few instances when she could have sworn someone was following her? She'd told the cops, right after the first break-in, and they'd just nodded. Nodded and said that without any evidence, they couldn't do a thing. They'd advised her to start taking a different route home from work. Told her to vary her walking routines. She had and the feeling of being watched, followed, had just persisted.

"Piper." Eric's eyes assessed her. "What is it?"

Ben edged closer. "Tell him or I will."

Back off, Ben. She'd confided this detail to him earlier, and he'd gone all nuclear on her. "I...thought that maybe someone was following me home from the gallery. Once or twice." More than that. "Actually, a few times. But whenever I look back, no one is ever there." Piper forced a shrug. "I'm probably just being jumpy."

Very slowly, Eric turned his head toward Ben. "You should have called me right away."

"Look, I only found out all the details after the second break-in! And she didn't want me to contact you, okay? I had to do it behind her back. You know how Piper gets about you! Shit, you make her nervous. Always have."

She backed up a step. "*She* is here. And like I said before, this case isn't what you usually handle, Eric. I got a new security system after the first break-in. I started making sure I left the gallery before dark. I took precautions."

Eric glanced around her place. "But he just got past the new system." He glowered. "You should have called me. My team could have installed it."

Right, yes, she got that he thought she'd made a mistake. "Would've, could've, should've, all right? But, look, dammit, the problem was that the alarm didn't even go off," she muttered. So much for the grand she'd paid having the system installed.

"You can't stay here until an updated system is in place. *My* system." Eric rolled back his shoulders. "So pack a bag. It's getting late, and you look dead on your feet."

Piper winced. "You always say the nicest things." She tugged at the edge of her shirt.

He blinked and cocked his head to the side. "Sorry. Should I have said...You look fucking gorgeous, but you're too pale, and I just saw you tremble so I want to get you the hell out of here? Would that work better for you?"

Her lips parted. She started to look at Ben—

Eric moved to the side, blocking her gaze. Forcing her to stare straight at him instead. "We're going to break that habit."

He'd lost her. "What are you even talking about?"

Eric smiled. A slow, lip-stretching smile that let her see the slash in his cheek.

A secret about his lip-stretching smile…it usually made her toes curl. And despite everything, her toes curled in her sneakers.

"Will you *please* get a bag ready, Piper?" Eric asked her.

Holy shit, he'd just said please.

"I'll do it," Ben announced helpfully. "And you can come home with me, Piper. I told you that already. Not like you haven't slept over at my place plenty of times. I don't know why you wouldn't stay last night." His feet padded over the floor as he headed toward her bedroom.

Eric seemed to have turned to stone. He stared at her. Just stared.

"Uh, Eric?" She almost waved her hand in front of his face.

He swallowed. His nostrils flared. Then he gave a nod. "You can stay with me. I've got plenty of room."

"I-I stayed in a motel last night."

"A *no-tell-motel*," Ben called out cheerfully — probably from her bedroom. "That place was creepy as hell. No way are you staying there again! *I* told you that already."

At Ben's shout, Eric turned on his heel and stalked down the hallway. Piper scrambled to keep up with him. As soon as they entered her bedroom, he stopped cold.

It was even more of a nightmare in there. Her mattress had been cut over and over, slashed. Her underwear was on the floor. Her jewelry box had been broken. Her clothes taken out of the closet. Some had been sliced, some thrown across the room.

"Sonofabitch." Eric's voice was a hard snarl of fury.

"The cops just left it this way." Ben shook his head as he bent to grab a pair of yoga pants from the floor. "Can you believe that?"

"They don't do clean-up." Each word from Eric seemed gritted out. "Just leave that stuff. We'll get her new things." He glanced toward Piper. "Those clothes are ruined."

Some of them could be saved, she was sure of it.

"I will take care of it," Eric promised her. "Consider it done already. You don't need to worry."

Weariness pulled at her. "It's so weird when you're nice. It creeps me out."

His lips twitched.

But then he looked around at her bedroom, and the faint amusement vanished instantly. "We're going home." He took her hand in his.

She tried not to jerk or flinch or give any sign that an electric current of heat had just shot through her fingers. That usually happened when he touched her. She got a bolt of sensual awareness. A bolt that made her heart quicken and her breath pant and her whole body tingle.

"Hey, wait! She can stay with me!" Ben bounded toward them, frowning. "I called you for your security expertise, but you don't need to take Piper home with you. I've got her."

"Not this time."

A furrow appeared between Ben's brows.

"Piper." Eric nodded toward her. "Can I speak with my brother for a moment? Alone?"

Seriously? "You want me to walk out of *my* bedroom so that you two can talk?" He wanted to kick her out of her own room?

"That would be great. Thank you," Eric added, as if he were trying to remember his manners.

She gaped for a moment. *Unbelievable.* Piper spun on her heel. Marched out.

The door clicked shut behind her.

***

The scent of lavender lingered in the air even after Piper left. Eric stood there a moment, every muscle in his body rock hard with tension. Rage surged inside of him, struggling to get out. When he thought about what had happened to Piper, to what the bastard had done to her things, about what the bastard could have done to Piper if *she'd* been there when he'd broken into her house—

Ben's hand clamped around his shoulder. "She isn't going home with you. Thanks for the help, I know you can get her the best security system, but I'll take her back with me. I'll—*ow!*"

Eric had grabbed his brother's hand. Grabbed his brother. And shoved Ben back against the door.

A sharp knock sounded. "Hey!" Piper's voice. "Everything okay in there?"

Ben stared at him with wide eyes.

"Fine!" Eric called back. "Just straightening a few things out." Some shit that should have been straightened out long ago.

"Are you crazy?" Ben whispered. "Like, I swear, I feared this day would come. All that work and no playtime routine that you have is not the way a human should live. Knew you were burning out your fuse."

"I thought you were fucking going to marry her."

Ben's eyes widened even more, nearly doubling in size. "Who?"

Don't kill your little brother. Don't kill him. "Piper." Eric's voice was low, meant only for Ben.

Shock flashed on Ben's face. "Why the hell would you think that?"

"Because you two have been inseparable for *years*. Because she sleeps over at your house '*all the time.*' Because you know practically every secret that she has, and she knows yours." He was clenching his back teeth. "I kept waiting for the day when you broke the news. Then you gave me the mystery call today. Told me I had to get to Piper's, ASAP. That you had something you needed to tell me." He'd heard all of that, and he'd nearly gone insane.

Why? Why?

Because I want Piper. He always had, dammit. Only he hadn't realized how completely, totally lost he was…until the moment came when he thought his brother was claiming her, forever.

"Uh, yeah, we're not getting married." Ben looked down at the hand Eric had slammed into his chest. "And you can get your hand off me, too."

"You just going to keep screwing around with her?" *Hell, no.* Eric shook his head. With his free hand, he flipped the lock on the door. "Fuck, no. The rules are changing."

Ben's mouth opened. Closed. Opened. The guy looked like a fish who'd been yanked out of the water. Then he finally mumbled, "I…haven't."

The words were so low that Eric almost missed them. "Come again?"

"I…I don't know where you got the idea, but Piper and I…we've *never* screwed around. She's my best friend."

The thunder of Eric's heartbeat seemed very, very loud. Too loud. "She was your first."

"*What in the fuck?*" Ben's voice wasn't low now. It was a yell.

Piper's footsteps rushed toward the closed door. "What is happening in there?"

"My brother is being crazy! And delusional!" Ben shouted. "That's what's happening."

No, he wasn't crazy. But Eric *was* tired of sitting back and not taking what he wanted. He'd had a serious wake-up call. If he didn't act, he *would* lose Piper.

"She's in danger," Eric snapped. "You know it or you wouldn't have called me. I can protect her in ways you never can. If some asshole is following her, if she's got a stalker, I will eliminate the threat. She needs me now." *Me, not you.*

It was Eric's turn. And he wasn't going to screw this up. Ben couldn't fix this problem for Piper, but Eric could. He *would.*

Ben's face showed his frustration. "She doesn't even like you."

An unfortunate situation he'd fix, hopefully. "I can keep her safe. My place is freaking Fort Knox, and you know it. Until we see exactly what we're dealing with, I need her with me."

Ben searched his gaze.

The door rattled behind him. "Did you lock the door?" Piper demanded. "Did you *lock* me out of my own bedroom?"

"*Don't you hurt her,*" Ben rasped.

"I never would."

Ben held his gaze a moment longer, then, finally, nodded.

Eric dropped his hand and stepped back. Ben began to move forward, but at the same instant, the door flew open. He stumbled when the door hit him in the back.

"I unlocked it from the outside!" Piper announced triumphantly. "Now what in the hell is going on?"

Ben raked a hand through his hair. "I want you to stay at Eric's tonight."

She bit her lower lip. "I have a motel room, and it's not really about what *you* want."

No, it wasn't. This was all about Piper. Hell, it had *always* been about Piper. "I don't want to scare you anymore than you already are," Eric began carefully.

Her long lashes flickered. She glanced at him, hitting him with the direct impact of her amazing eyes. Gold and gorgeous. Golden eyes, golden skin, and silky, golden hair that fell just below her chin.

"The cops are overworked and understaffed." A sad truth. "And if there wasn't evidence left behind, if this guy covered his tracks and didn't leave prints, but still left a wake of destruction, you *know* that's bad news."

She tugged on her left ear. Ever since she'd been a kid, she'd done that exact move whenever she was afraid. The first time he'd seen her do it, she'd been nine. Some asshole punk had been standing over her, yelling at Piper that he wanted her lunch money.

So Eric had tackled the kid.

Piper had gone skipping away with Ben. But later, she'd used her lunch money to buy Eric a thank you ice cream. Chocolate, his favorite. Because Piper always seemed to know what he liked.

Except when it came to one area in particular…

"I have four freaking guest rooms," he growled when she tugged on her ear again. "Not like I'm asking you to share my bed."

She gave him a look of such utter horror…

Eric's back teeth clenched.

"It's a good idea, Piper," Ben said, voice grudging.

Her full lips parted.

"Not the sharing his bed part," Ben rushed to add. "Dear God, never that. Hell, no."

He should punch the bastard. Blood relation or not.

"But he does have plenty of room and the best security." Ben raked a hand through his hair. "And I'm worried or I never would have called him in the first place. You're worried, too. If some freak is out there, watching you, do you really want to be alone in some cheap motel with a flimsy lock?"

Piper shook her head. "No, no, I don't." She squared her delicate shoulders as her gaze lingered on Eric. "But how long are we talking here? I don't want to inconvenience you."

She would never be an inconvenience.

"And what would your girlfriend think about me staying at your place?"

Girlfriend?

"What girlfriend?" Ben burst out with a laugh before Eric could respond. "You know he's a flavor-of-the-week kind of guy. He has sex with them, then he moves on."

Eric was going to kill his brother. Murder him and hide the body so well that no one would ever find the remains. "That's not what I fucking do." Was that what Piper thought he was like? Well, shit, what kind of trash had his kid brother told her over the years?

"I-I don't want to know about your sex life." Piper's cheeks turned a soft pink. "No need to overshare."

She did need to know about it. Just as he sure as hell wanted to know about hers. "Is there a lover who is going to come looking for you?"

If she looked at Ben…

But Piper kept her gaze on Eric. "I'm not involved with anyone right now."

Hell, yes. "Perfect." He didn't need to kick anyone's ass. Because a lover should sure as shit be there keeping her safe.

But Piper frowned at his response.

Oh, wait, had he spoken with too much satisfaction? He'd have to be more careful. Eric sauntered forward and took her hand. "I'll have a crew over here first thing in the morning. For now, come with me and get some rest. You're dead on your feet."

And, wonder of wonders, Piper gave a nod. "Okay. Thank you."

He realized just how terrified she must be. Because Piper never gave in on anything.

Ben's hand clamped around his shoulder. "I'll lock up here."

Eric glanced at his brother.

Ben's bright gaze was suspicious. "And you *will* take care of her? You'll be on your best behavior?"

What was he? Six? Best behavior, his ass. "I've got her." A brisk nod. Eric tightened his hold on Piper and led her out of the house. Darkness reigned outside. No stars glittered overhead because heavy clouds had moved in. A dank cold settled around them, and when Piper shivered, he immediately shouldered off his coat and put it around her shoulders.

She started to head for her car.

"Let me take you."

Frowning, she peered at him. "I need my own wheels."

He was being far too cautious, he knew it, but...*this was Piper.* "I want a member of my team to go over your ride." He cast a quick glance at the red convertible. "Do a sweep on it, make sure everything is okay." He was trying not to scare her, but he also didn't want to take any chances.

"What is it that you think is wrong with my car?" She bit her lower lip as she waited for his response.

Such a delectable lip.

"If you feel like you've been followed, maybe someone is keeping tabs on you. Wouldn't be hard to hide a device on your vehicle, one that would transmit GPS coordinates back to the SOB who put it there. Everywhere you went, he'd know about it." A pause. "You said you were out of town when both break-ins occurred."

"Yes."

"Did you drive out of town? Or fly?"

"Drove. Both times."

"So maybe he knew you were out of town because he'd been watching your house." His gaze darted down the dark street. "Or because he was tracking your car. Either way, I'd feel better leaving it here. No sense taking chances."

"Dammit, I *hate* this."

His body brushed against hers. "I will protect you. I swear it." God, he wanted to kiss her. To drop his mouth to hers and taste her. But he was trying to show her that she needed him. He had to play this right. *Step back.*

His car waited in front of her driveway, and he opened the passenger side door for her. Her body slid against his, the scent of lavender teased him, and Eric pulled in a deep breath.

When she was settled into the seat, Piper glanced up at him. The interior light from the vehicle shone down on her, giving him a perfect view of her. High cheekbones. Slightly pointed chin—the stubborn chin that always notched up when she got angry with him. Her full, red lips. Her incredible eyes. Eyes that appeared…worried.

"Eric, you don't think someone is watching me right now, do you?"

He stiffened. Then he forced a smile. "You're safe with me, Piper. Just remember that." He shut her door and walked around the car, and as he did, his gaze cut toward the darkness.

Was someone watching Piper?

Was someone planning to hurt her?

If so…Eric would fucking destroy the bastard.

CHAPTER TWO

A woman didn't normally expect the villain of her childhood and teenage years to suddenly start playing the hero of the story, so Piper couldn't quite make herself relax as Eric drove them back to his home. He lived in a fancy Atlanta suburb, one of those high-end, way-behind-a-gate places. His house definitely qualified as a mansion. His family had always possessed money, but Eric had exploded with his security corporation. After he'd graduated from MIT, the guy had created some sort of new security tech that had taken the world by storm. In the blink of an eye, he'd suddenly had the rich and famous banging at his door. And things had only been getting started for him.

"I can't believe you live in this place all alone." She leaned forward and peered up at the sprawling estate. Tuxedo Park. Talk about old money and too much power. The circular driveway led toward the English-style manor. An actual manor. Lights shone from within, providing a soft glow as tall, swaying pines surrounded the home.

"I'm not always alone."

Even though heat poured from the vents in the car, she still shivered. Probably because of his deep, dark voice. Or maybe because she was running on fumes. Either way, she was not really up to her normal snark level with Eric.

And, of course, the guy wasn't always alone. He had his flavors of the week, didn't he? Ben had certainly told her enough stories about them over the years.

But maybe she should just leave all of the bullshit behind. Maybe... "For once, can we just be normal people?"

He braked. Turned off the Benz. She felt his stare on her.

"I thought we were normal."

"I mean...can you stop hating me and I'll stop baiting you, and we can just get through this night without any trouble? I'm truly grateful for your help, and I just..." Her words floundered because she didn't know what to say.

"You're dead wrong."

Her head jerked toward him.

"I don't hate you. Never have." A pause. "Why would you think that?"

Was he serious? "Because you avoid me! You have for years! If I come into a room, you leave it. You stare at me and a muscle jerks in your jaw. When I was a sixteen, I heard you telling Ben that I shouldn't come over to swim anymore, that you didn't want me there." Okay, she needed to pull back. She'd just gotten a wee bit out of control. All that pent-up hostility. When it came to Eric, she certainly felt *pent-up*. "Look, I'm trying not to fight." Their fights typically just happened. She never tried to start them. "Can we just go inside and I'll head into a guest room? You won't see me for the rest of the night. Promise."

He opened his car door. She shoved open the passenger door, not waiting for him to come around and open it. He'd do that, she knew he would. She'd always seen him open doors for his dates over the years. He could be so gentlemanly one moment, but then be a total jerk to her and Ben the next.

Mood swings. He had them.

He met her on the stone steps that led to the manor. "You're not sixteen anymore."

No, she wasn't.

"And for the record, hate is the last thing I feel for you. I rather thought you would have figured that out by now."

"When it comes to you, I have a hard time figuring out most things." She was still wearing his coat. It smelled like him. All crisp and masculine and a little bit awesome.

Focus.

He unlocked the front door, typed in his security code, and waved her inside. She walked past him, being extra careful *not* to let her body brush against his. She'd actually never been in his house before. He'd never invited her over.

Because they weren't besties. That would be her and Ben. She should have gone to his place. Why hadn't she?

"I have security cameras that monitor the perimeter of the property. Motion sensors are turned on, and a floodlight system activates when they are triggered." He motioned to a door on the right. "That's my monitor room. You can go in there and access all of the security feeds. No one will get to this house without me being aware of it, I promise."

Right. And *that* was why she'd gone with Eric instead of dear old Ben.

Eric had already shut the door. He reset his alarm, and she stood there, shifting a bit nervously in the massive foyer. The ceiling was up at least two stories, and a bright chandelier glittered down on her.

"Where is the guest room?" Piper asked as she rocked onto the balls of her sneakered feet.

"I'll show you. Come this way."

She shrugged out of his coat and offered it to him. "I don't need this any longer."

He took the coat, but their fingers brushed and—*dammit.* The spark was there again.

Only this time, he was staring straight in her eyes when she felt the spark. And with a sinking heart, Piper realized—

"You feel it," Eric murmured.

Oh, shit.

"But then, I figured you must. After all, that kiss we had was something, wasn't it?"

He had not just referenced the kiss. The kiss that she had begged him to never, ever talk about. A kiss he'd sworn to keep secret.

"Did Ben ever find out about that?" Eric asked her as he tilted his head and studied her with his dark, deep eyes. "Or does he still think he was your first?"

She stared at him for a moment. Just stared. Then she smiled. "Okay, then." Piper gave a firm nod before she turned on her heel and reached for the doorknob. "I'll just be on my way."

"*Piper.*"

His hand closed around her wrist.

"You are such an ass," she told him, meaning the words with every fiber of her being. He'd promised to never bring up the kiss. *Promised.*

"I know I am. Mostly because I'm a jealous dumbass when it comes to you."

He was jealous? Since when? She turned her head and squinted at him. If he was mocking her, she was so not in the mood.

"It's been a really shitty night," he muttered. "You don't know what it was like when I thought—the call from him…" But his voice just trailed off.

Piper rolled her eyes. "Shitty night. Check. Because someone broke into your home and wrecked all of your things? Slashed your underwear? Scared the crap out of you?" She let mock surprise flash on her face as she stared at him. "Oh, wait, no, that was me."

He flushed. "I'm sorry. I'll show you to the guest room. Just follow me." He turned and started doing his silent walk away routine.

She was bone-weary, scared, and frustrated. Piper was pretty sure it was close to eleven PM, and she just wanted to collapse. For the moment, she decided to simply take the guest room.

Yet as she climbed up the spiral staircase after him, she remembered what he'd said at her place. The guy had thought she and Ben were going to reveal big, romantic news. "Why would you care if Ben and I did get married? I mean, what's your deal? Do you think I'm not good enough for him?" And that *hurt.*

Her family had never possessed as much money as Eric's did. Especially after her father had cut out. When he'd bailed, she and her mother had pretty much lost everything. She'd only been able to stay in her private school because of a scholarship, one that she strongly suspected had come straight from the Wilde family. No, she'd never been on their financial level, but that hadn't seemed to matter. Ben and Eric—their parents weren't stuffy or pretentious. They'd opened their home to her from day one. Pre-K, day one.

Only Eric had seemed to be unwelcoming over the years.

Now she was in *his* house.

At her words, he stopped on the stairs. Angled toward her. "On the contrary, I think you're too good for my brother. Far too good."

Now she was surprised.

"I think you're too good for any of the jerks who've tried to be with you."

Her stomach was in knots. "When you say nice things, it makes me worry." She'd told him that before. No, maybe she'd said that he creeped her out. Both were true.

A half-smile curved his lips as he turned away once more. He didn't speak again, not until they'd climbed the stairs, strolled down a hallway, and paused in front of a white door. "This is your room. It connects to a private bath. There should be an extra robe inside the bathroom, and if you need anything else, just let me know."

She nibbled on her lower lip. "Where will you be?"

His gaze cut to the side. As in…the door right beside hers.

Uh, oh. "*That's* your room?"

A nod. "If you want me, all you have to do is call out."

Want me. "I'll be fine." She reached for the doorknob.

"I will find him, Piper."

If anyone could, it would be Eric. Despite their personal differences, she knew he was good at his job. He tracked celebrity stalkers, he found missing children, he created security systems to protect the most valuable items in the world — the guy made the headlines every other day.

He could find the jerk who was making her life hell.

"Why is this happening?" She shook her head. "There was so much rage in my house." Part of her guard lowered, for just a moment, as she looked at him. "I could feel it, you know? He *destroyed* my things. Smashed all of the photos of me and Ben. Of me and all my friends. He slashed my paintings. Ripped up my clothes." She shook her head. "But I don't think he took *anything*. He just destroyed stuff. That's why the cops — I don't know, maybe that's why they couldn't do much. It wasn't a burglary. It wasn't an attack on me. It wasn't—"

He moved closer. "It was an attack on you." Suddenly, he seemed very, very serious. "And, yes, I could feel the rage, that's what worries me. The guy is fixated. He destroyed the things that mattered to you because I think he wanted to *hurt* you. I've seen stalkers escalate. That's what I'm worried this guy is doing. First, he broke into your house and just moved some things around."

"Why? Why did he do that?"

"Because he wanted to feel close to you. Because touching your things, being in your home, being in your *bedroom*, made him feel like he had an intimate connection to you. That's how those guys operate."

Oh, God. She shook her head.

"He waited, and he may have watched you."

Her lips pressed together.

"Those times you felt as if someone was there? Maybe he was. He could have watched, and he could have wanted you more."

She couldn't look away from his eyes.

"Sometimes," Eric said, his voice careful, "you can get caught up in a fantasy. You can lose track of reality, and you can decide that you'll do *anything* to make your fantasy come true. He could have thought that you were his. But then something happened. Maybe he saw you with another man. Maybe *something* broke his fantasy, and he struck out."

She swallowed. "He wanted to hurt me, so he destroyed my things?"

"I've seen it before." A pause. "And I've seen it become worse. Because the next step—" He stopped.

Too late. "The next step—would that be hurting me?" No, no, *no*.

His eyes were so dark and deep. "I'm not going to let that happen."

"I haven't done anything." Her voice rose. She sucked in a breath. *Get your control back. Get it back.* "I've been working and doing my job. Why is someone fixated on me? Why is someone doing this to me?"

He shook his head.

"And why are you so quick to help me?" The last question came out too softly. "Especially when I thought you hated me." It was because her emotions were so raw — *that* was why she'd just let the last part slip out.

His eyes widened. Then he stepped toward her. He eliminated the space between them and caged her with his body. Growing up, Eric Wilde had been the rock star of her little world. He'd been the star of every single freaking sport in the school, and he'd been valedictorian. There had been nothing he couldn't do, and he'd always made it clear that she was an annoyance in his life. The girl who tagged around with his little brother and got in the way. She'd been younger than Eric by two years. Two years shouldn't have mattered much, but, back then, they had.

"Hate is not what I feel for you." His gaze dropped to her mouth.

He was staring at her mouth like…oh, no. No way. Her hands flew up. Her intention had been to put her hands on his chest and push him back. But when she touched him, when she felt the strength of his muscles through the shirt and the heat of his body, Piper didn't shove him back.

How much does the guy work out?

His jaw hardened. "We're going to need to clear the air between us very soon, Piper. Very, very soon. Because I'm not standing back any longer. There's too much to lose."

There always had been.

"Get some rest. We'll talk in the morning." His eyes were still on her mouth.

And she was still touching him.

Coming to his place had been a serious mistake. She'd stay the one night—just the one—and then other arrangements had to be made.

"Do you ever think about it?" Eric asked, voice all deep and dark and rumbling.

Her gaze had zeroed in on his mouth. At his words, her stare whipped right back up.

"Our kiss? Your *first* kiss? Do you think about it?"

She shook her head. It was easier to lie if you didn't have to speak. She'd learned that long ago. When she spoke and told a lie, her voice always cracked. So, it was much better for her to just stay silent.

"I liked being your first."

Push him away.

She did not want to remember their kiss. That long ago, stupid mistake. She'd been fifteen, he'd been seventeen. It had been raining, and they'd gotten stuck at school. She'd been working on an art project—like always—and, hell, she had no idea why he'd stayed so late that day. Maybe basketball practice or something? But she'd gone outside and instead of walking home, she'd stood underneath the overhang as the rain had poured down. She'd been trying to wait out the storm.

Then she'd turned around and Eric had been there.

"Piper?"

She swallowed. "I don't see the point in talking about mistakes." Her voice didn't crack. She wasn't lying. It *had* been a mistake. And one of the few secrets that she'd never told Ben. "Good night." Now her hand did push against his chest.

He backed up. Turned away.

She could breathe again.

Until he glanced back at her, a faint smile on his face. "Funny. That mistake was the best kiss of my life."

She actually felt the shock roll through her. No way. He had not just said—

"Of course, I could be mistaken. It was a hell of a long time ago. Maybe we should try again one day. See if the present is better than the past." He winked at her. "Or maybe you've gotten even better since then."

She felt pinpricks in her face.

Then Eric laughed. "Or maybe you're a lot worse. You'll have to show me."

Show him? Glaring, she flipped him off and stormed into the guest room. Piper slammed the door to *show* him how she really felt. The guy had been the bane of her existence for too long. And now she was counting on him for help? For protection?

Growling, she yanked off her shirt as she stalked toward the bathroom. The situation totally sucked.

And...

Dammit, that stupid kiss had been the best of her life, too.

***

He was a world-class liar. Always had been. But Eric hadn't been lying to Piper, and it was a fucking sad thing to admit, but when he'd been seventeen and he'd kissed her...

Hell, yes, that kiss had been incredible.

He raked a hand over his face as he headed toward his room. Piper Lane was in his house. *Piper Lane.*

He kicked the bedroom door shut and hauled out his phone. He didn't care what time it was, he needed to get his crew started on her case. He dialed his Vice President and had Simon Forrest on the line in moments.

"You are totally interrupting something very, very important," Simon growled at him. "Why is your timing always shit?"

"I want our best men sent to Piper Lane's home first thing in the morning. She's had two break-ins, and some SOB trashed her place."

"What?" Simon's voice sharpened. "Ben's Piper?"

Eric nearly crushed the phone. *She isn't Ben's.*

"Is she okay?" Simon demanded.

"She's fine. She's here."

Silence. Then... "Want to say that again?"

He knew the guy had heard him perfectly the first time. "She's staying at my place until we can catch this bastard. The local PD is overwhelmed, and I won't have her put in danger. I want the best team we have doing a full security installation at her place, but before that, I want the area swept for any evidence that might have been left behind." He exhaled. "And I want a complete sweep on her car. Check for any GPS devices and make sure that baby is running perfectly." Sabotaging a car would be an easy way to hurt a target.

"Uh, sure thing, buddy, but if the cops have already been to her place…"

"I want the place examined again." Cold fury punctuated the words. "And we both know that our team is the best in the whole state." Actually, the best on the entire East Coast.

Simon didn't argue.

"She's scared," Eric added grimly. "And I told her we'd find this jerk. He isn't going to get close to her."

A pause, then…"This sounds personal."

He looked toward the wall that separated him from Piper's bedroom. "It is."

***

Piper wasn't home. Her house was dark and silent. Her car sat in the driveway, a cute little red convertible.

Piper liked flash. She liked fun. She had a laugh that lit up a room. And when she looked at him, when her golden eyes locked on his…

He could see straight into her soul.

He'd been waiting on Piper for a long time. Waiting for someone like her to come into his life. Someone to quiet the demons inside. She'd been waiting for him, too. He knew it.

His gloved fingers trailed along the front of her car. Where had Piper gone? It was after midnight, no cops were around, and her home just sat, so cold and alone.

A slow anger churned inside of him.

Where the hell did you go, Piper?

And…

Who was she with?

CHAPTER THREE

The stair creaked beneath her bare toes. Piper froze at the sound, then glanced quickly over her shoulder. The area at the top of the stairs was still dark. No sign of Eric.

Good. The last thing she wanted was for him to find her raiding his refrigerator. But, well, a woman had to do what a woman had to do.

She'd tried to go to sleep. But she'd just tossed and turned and stared at the ceiling. And then she'd realized that she hadn't eaten since lunch. Hunger was keeping her awake. And fear. But she couldn't do much about the fear, not right then.

The hunger, however, was a problem that she could tackle.

When she reached the landing, Piper peered to the left and then to the right. A tour of the house would have made things easier, but Piper figured she could blunder her way around. She opened the door to the right.

A lamp had been left on inside that room, and it spilled onto the massive book cases. Onto the desk. The leather chairs.

Eric's office.

Her hand tightened on the doorknob. She could see a few picture frames on his desk. The whole room just looked so *normal*. Was that a football tossed in his chair? She was pretty sure he had some kind of framed baseball bat hanging on the wall.

Piper inched closer, narrowing her eyes so that she could see better. Ah, right. A bat from the Atlanta Braves. She took a few more steps toward the framed bat. Looked like he'd gotten the whole team to autograph it for him.

Figured.

"What are you doing?"

She jumped and whirled around, and her hip bumped into the side of his desk. When she hit it, one of the framed photographs tumbled off the edge and hit the floor with a hard thunk.

"Century, study lights on," Eric announced, and the overhead lights flashed on. Immediately, she went from being in a dimly lit, one lamp room, to a full-on *bright* world. Piper blinked frantically as her eyes adjusted to the flood of illumination.

"Piper?" Eric crossed his arms over his chest and propped one broad shoulder against the doorframe. "What the hell are you doing?"

She grabbed for the fallen picture frame. "Getting something to eat."

He frowned at her. "This isn't the kitchen."

"Yes, ahem..." Piper cleared her throat. "I missed the tour of the house, so I was trying to find..." But her voice trailed away. She'd just gotten a look at the photo in the frame. It was a photo of her. One in which she was grinning from ear to ear. She had her arm looped around Ben's shoulders. "Why do you have a picture of me?" Her head whipped up as she gaped at him.

He sighed. His arms dropped, and he started his slow, silent stroll toward her. "It's a picture of you and my *brother*." Eric reached for the frame.

His fingers slid over hers. Was that deliberate? The quick jump of her heart said the move had been.

"You could have cut me out," she mumbled. Why hadn't he? Piper shook her head. He was confusing her so much. The last time they'd seen each other—a few weeks back at Christmas— he'd barely talked to her at all when he'd arrived at Ben's holiday party. Of course, Eric's supermodel of the moment had been at his side.

He usually had someone at his side.

"Why would I cut you out?" Now he looked genuinely perplexed.

She let go of the photo. There was no need for an undignified tug-of-war. "I'm not family."

His eyes were on her. "No, you sure as hell aren't."

Why did that *hurt*? Why did she still let anything he said hurt her? Why had she always been too sensitive where Eric was concerned?

He put the frame back on his desk. Then his gaze drifted over her. "You…look…um…"

"The robe was in the bathroom. I guess one of your exes left it there?" And she felt way creeped out wearing a castoff. "Could I get something else? Like, do you have an old t-shirt or something I could borrow?" The robe was silk, a pale blue, and it hung to mid-thigh. It was sexy. Seductive. And so not her.

He swallowed. His eyes rose to meet hers. "Yeah, yeah, I have something." And he started unbuttoning the white button-down that he wore.

Eric had sauntered into the study wearing loose jeans and a white button-down shirt. The long sleeves were undone at his wrists. She doubted that he'd gone to bed at all. And, now, apparently, he was stripping for her.

"You don't need to do—" Piper stopped. He'd undone half of the buttons, baring his upper chest. As she watched, the shirt parted even more, and she glimpsed his amazing abs. All of those gorgeous muscles.

He finished unbuttoning the shirt, and he slid it off his shoulders. She was still staring at his chest. His six-pack. Twelve pack?

"How much do you work out?" *Oh, no.* Her question had been out-loud. She had a tendency to blurt the wrong things to Eric. Story of her life.

He gave her a slow smile. Slow and toe-curling. He also held out his shirt to her. "Your turn."

"What?"

"You don't like the robe?" A shrug. "Go ahead and change. Here's a shirt for you."

She snatched the shirt from him. "I'm not changing in front of you."

"Pity. But a guy can dream." He shrugged. "Want me to turn my back? I mean, if the robe is bothering you that much, I can turn around and you can change, no problem."

"Do you even know who left the robe?"

He cocked a brow. She took that to mean that, no, he had zero clue.

Ugh. "Just turn around."

He spun around, giving her a view of his powerful back and muscled shoulders. Those shoulders—he'd been a great linebacker, back in the day.

She dropped the robe. It hit the floor with a flutter of silk. Piper still had on her panties and bra—white cotton, simple—and she hurriedly slid her arms into the shirt. Of course, the thing was huge, and it carried Eric's crisp scent. Her fingers fumbled a little as she hurriedly buttoned the shirt. The garment covered more of her than the robe had, so she figured that was something. "Okay, I'm good."

He slowly turned toward her. His gaze started at her head, then fell slowly down her body. "Far better than good."

She was rolling up one of the sleeves. At his words, her eyes narrowed suspiciously.

Eric cleared his throat. "If the goal was to look less sexy, you totally failed. Sorry."

"That wasn't the goal."

Now both brows rose. "You wanted to look sexier? Mission accomplished."

Her cheeks burned. "I wanted something less...leftover."

All humor left his face. "It won't happen again. My apologies." He turned on his heel. Headed for the door. "I'll show you to the kitchen. You can eat anything you want."

That was it? She took a step forward, then glanced at the robe. "What about—"

"Just leave it. You're hungry. Let's deal with that now. I'll take care of the robe later."

Okay. She hurried after him, double-timing her steps because the guy was moving fast. They rounded a few corners, headed down a hallway, and then—

"Century, kitchen lights on," Eric announced.

Lights flashed on in the kitchen. A massive kitchen. Gleaming white granite countertops. Four sinks. Two ovens. Two refrigerators. Why on earth would one person ever need so much?

"Century is my security system."

Yes, she'd figured that out.

"What's your pleasure, Piper?"

Her gaze swung to him. "I, um, was just looking for a late-night snack." She tucked a lock of hair behind her ear and tugged on the lobe.

His lips pressed together. "Got just the thing." He opened the fridge—no, the freezer—and pulled out a gallon of ice cream. "Still like chocolate chip cookie dough?"

God, yes. She reached for the ice cream.

Eric laughed. "Have a seat at the bar. I'll get you a spoon."

She hopped up on the barstool, his shirt inching up her thighs. He opened a drawer, rifled around, and then paced toward her with not one, but two spoons.

"You in the mood to share?"

Not really. "Since when do you like anything but chocolate?"

A shrug. "A guy has to be open to new experiences."

Okay. His house, his ice cream, so she had to share.

He slid onto the bar stool next to her, put the ice cream between them, and offered her a spoon. Suddenly feeling nervous, she hesitated.

"I'm not going to bite, Piper."

Of course, not.

She reached for the spoon.

"Unless you'd like me to."

Her gaze shot to his. There was absolutely no mistaking the desire in his eyes. Hot, dark. Consuming.

She snatched the spoon from him. Then she thrust it into the ice cream, scooped up a ton, and shoved it into her mouth.

Maybe that would cool her down.

Because the way he was looking at her…

"My timing is shit, isn't it?" He scooped up a helping of ice cream. Slid it into his mouth. Savored it a moment. "I'm supposed to be making you feel safe and reassured because I know you're going through a nightmare. And I just hit on you."

She swallowed. "You didn't mean it." He *never* meant it. Wasn't that his deal? Piper took another spoonful of ice cream and actually managed to taste the deliciousness this time. He hadn't meant it when he'd kissed her so long ago. The very next day, he'd been with someone else. He hadn't meant it any of the times that he'd flirted with her over the years. The random times. "It's just a game you play with me."

She felt him stiffen.

Piper took another spoonful of ice cream. The company might be stressing her, but the ice cream was heavenly.

"You are not a game."

She licked away a little bit of ice cream that had gotten left behind on the spoon. And then her gaze darted to him.

"Is that what you think, Piper? That I've been playing some game with you all these years?"

Another dip into the ice cream. Another quick taste. A moment to pull up her courage and… "What else could it be?"

"What else, indeed?"

Her breath whispered out. She took another lick on the spoon.

His attention remained on her. Oh, damn, but he was sexy. Those loose jeans, those abs, the way his tousled hair slid over his forehead...the stubble on his jaw.

Sexy. Trouble.

Bad news.

"This was such a mistake." She put down her spoon. "Maybe...can you just refer me to one of your agents in the morning? I know you don't do field work yourself. I can talk with him—or her, definitely, preferably *her*—and get my, ah, situation handled." She'd stay through the night at Eric's place, but she'd head out at first light.

Piper slid off the stool and pushed away from the bar—

Eric's fingers curled around her wrist. "I screw up with you all the time, don't I? It's an old habit, but one I intend to try like hell to break."

"This was a—"

His hold tightened. "It *wasn't* a mistake. You need help, and I am going to help you. There are no strings attached to what I am doing. My team will secure your place. We'll figure out who is messing with you, and you will be safe, Piper. Count on it." He'd put down his spoon before he'd grabbed her. His hand was big and powerful, but he wasn't hurting her or anything. He'd always been careful when they touched. The guy was strong, but always completely in control.

That was Eric.

He blew out a long breath. "I need to ask you something. I think it would be good, just to clear the air. So that I can know where I stand."

"Okay." She didn't like this.

His thumb stroked along her inner wrist, and her traitorous pulse jumped.

Stay cool. Stay focused. "What's the question?"

"Do you want me, Piper? Are you attracted to me at all?"

***

It was easy enough to get inside Piper's house. He'd been in there several times already. Once, he'd even gone inside when she'd been sleeping. She'd been in the bed, tangled in the covers, wearing a pair of jogging shorts and a blue t-shirt. She'd been beautiful. He'd watched her. Thought about touching her.

But hadn't. That time, he'd left her sleeping. Left her to her dreams. Maybe she'd even dreamed of him.

Now, he slipped into her bedroom. The cops had been there. She'd called them, let them search her place, but he knew that they wouldn't turn up anything. There was nothing to find.

Her home was a safe space for Piper. Or at least, that was what she'd thought. He wanted her to see that she was wrong. The safety net she had around herself — it was just an illusion.

The world wasn't a safe place. It was dangerous and dark. And deadly.

He lifted the gas can that he'd brought with him. And then he poured it onto her bed.

CHAPTER FOUR

If Piper told him that she didn't want him, then Eric was going to back the fuck off. He didn't want to play games. Dammit, is that what she thought he'd been doing? Playing with her? Hell, no.

No games. Not when it came to her.

He just wanted to be clear. He wanted to put everything on the table. Find out where he stood. Where she did. This talk between them was long overdue.

*And if she says to screw off...*Then that was her choice.

"Piper?" Eric forced out her name when she simply stared at him with her incredible eyes.

"Why are you asking me this?"

"Because I want to know." *No, give her the truth.* "Because I've wanted you for a very, very long time, and I'm tired of pretending that I don't. I get that my timing is shit. I get that, believe me. But I wanted you to know—dammit, I just—"

"You want me?" She shook her head. "Since when?"

Since you were fifteen. Since I waited after school for you because I didn't want you walking home alone. Since it started raining and your hair was slick against your cheek, and I went to brush it back and I wound up kissing you. She wasn't ready for all that.

Neither was he.

Baby steps. Baby freaking steps. Eric cleared his throat. "For a long time."

She looked away. She wasn't going to answer him. Or, hell, maybe her silence was an answer. He'd back off. He'd—

"Yes." So soft.

He blinked.

She tugged on her hand. "Let me go."

He did. Immediately.

"I am attracted to you. It's obvious, I'm sure. It's probably been obvious for quite some time." She backed away from him. Her face was solemn. A little sad, and he didn't want that. He'd never liked it when Piper was sad.

Usually Ben swept in when she was sad and made her feel better.

Fuck him.

He could do this. Eric knew that he could make her happy. If she would just give him the chance.

"But we…" She gestured back and forth between them. "We're a mistake. You told me that yourself, remember? Back when we were just kids. We're total opposites and…there's your brother." Her smile didn't reach her eyes. "There is always your brother." Piper turned from him.

He watched her walk away from him, as she'd left him so many times. Usually after he made some dumbass remark to her. Only this time, he couldn't stay silent as she left him. "You think I like being desperate for my brother's lover?"

Her shoulders stiffened.

"You think that's a line I want to cross? You think I haven't tried to stay the hell away from you for *years?*"

She peeked over her shoulder at him. Her expression was shocked then, in a blink, guarded. Totally guarded. Piper was never guarded. She wore her emotions on her sleeve.

You started this thing. Don't stop now. Eric sucked in a breath. "What do you think I've been doing all this time? You and Ben—you've been inseparable since the first grade."

"Pre-K."

Dammit! He tried to find the right words. "I get that you were his first."

Her eyes widened.

"And I waited. I backed the hell off. Time passed, and I didn't do *anything.* Every time you came near me, I'd want you again, but I didn't say a word. The two of you—I kept thinking one of these days, *one of these freaking days,* I'll get the phone call telling me that you and Ben are getting married. I knew that when the call came, I'd have to drag my ass over to you. Have to smile and act like I was thrilled for you both. When the truth of the matter is…"

She turned toward him, facing him fully. Wearing *his* shirt and looking so sexy that she made him ache. "The truth?"

"The truth is that the day Ben puts a ring on your finger, I might very well knock his ass out."

She looked down at her left hand. Wiggled her fingers. "There's no ring here." Her hair slid over her cheek as she peered back at him. "But you thought that is what happened tonight, didn't you? You said that, back at my place."

Eric gave a jerky nod.

"And you still came over…to knock out Ben?"

He didn't know what the hell he'd planned to do at her place. Keep his mouth shut? Congratulate his brother? But when he'd gotten there… "You weren't engaged. The two of you were still doing your dance."

She shook her head.

"I get that he was your first lover, but first doesn't give him forever." His fingers flexed and clenched at his sides. "And I've decided that I've waited long enough. Ben will fucking hate me, but I am tired of holding back. If there is a chance that you want me, I want to take that chance." *I want to take you.*

There. He'd done it. Burned every bridge that he had.

And Piper just...stared at him.

He swore that the room got so quiet that he could even hear the ticking of the big clock on the wall. He hated that clock. An interior decorator had installed it. He'd be trashing it come dawn.

The minutes stretched by.

She wasn't going to say anything. And the ice cream was melting on the bar. He grabbed it, shoved it back into the freezer—

"This is the second time you mentioned that I was Ben's first."

He slammed the freezer shut. That had been his biggest damn problem. He'd heard Ben make that confession two months after Eric had kissed Piper. Two freaking months.

"I think you're confused."

He looked at her. Her hands were twisted in front of her.

"I've never slept with Ben. He's my best friend. Sleeping with him would just screw things up. Not make anything better. I value what I have with him too much to lose it for sex."

Holy fuck. Holy ever-loving... "Your voice didn't crack."

She frowned at him.

Shock rolled through his body. "You haven't slept with my brother?"

"No, I have *not* slept with Ben."

The drumming of his heartbeat quickened. "You've stayed at his house. He said that shit tonight. I *know*—"

"On his couch, when we'd been out drinking because I didn't want to drive home. I crashed at his place during college, too. He crashed at mine. It just became a habit after a while. It's what happens between friends."

He was going to kill Ben. "I heard him say…he damn well *said* you'd been his first."

Her lips pressed together, and her eyelids flickered. "I don't know when you heard him say that or who he was talking to, but I am telling you right here and now that I have never slept with Ben. Believe me or not, it's your choice."

Eric's breath burned in his lungs. He'd stayed away from her for *years,* been tormented by the idea of them together and there was—

No reason. No reason at all to hold back.

"For the record, I'm not sleeping with anyone right now. I'm not involved with anyone," she added, blushing a little.

"Neither am I." He took a step toward her.

She didn't back up.

"I'm not your best friend, Piper." His voice was gravel rough. Too hard and rumbling but he couldn't help that. "You don't have to worry about screwing up a friendship with me."

Her lips twitched. "I guess there is that…bonus?"

"I want you."

Her gaze drifted down his chest.

"You're not telling me to fuck off." He kept advancing on her. The dream he'd had forever—

right in front of him. "You're not hauling ass out of this kitchen."

"No."

"Why not?" He stopped in front of her, and Eric just had to touch her. His hand lifted, and his fingers caressed her cheek. Her silken, smooth cheek.

"Because I remember the kiss." Her lashes flickered. "I also remember how much it hurt when you turned your back on me the next day."

No, it hadn't been like that—

"But I'm not fifteen. You're not seventeen. We're adults, and maybe…maybe I want to see if the kiss would still be as good. Maybe it's time for us both to find out." Her head tilted back. "It's a kiss. One kiss. What could it hurt? I mean, we could kiss and realize we don't have any real attraction. That nothing is between us."

Bullshit. He wanted her so much his whole body ached. He woke up at night because dreams of her tormented him.

"Let's just see what happens. Me and you." Her gaze searched his. "No strings. No promises. Just a kiss."

His hand slid under her hair. He leaned over her. She was small, barely over five feet two inches, and he towered over six feet. He'd always known he'd have to be careful with her. Use extra care.

Treat her with all the tenderness he possessed…a hard feat, considering how savagely he wanted her.

"We don't tell Ben about this," she whispered. "Not yet, I mean. It's just a kiss."

His lips pressed to hers. Softly. Carefully. And…

Her mouth opened for him. Her tongue touched his.

Desire erupted.

Just a kiss.

He tasted her, he savored her, and he went wild for her. Her hands curled around his shoulders as she pulled him closer. He could feel her breasts pressing against him. The soft curves. The tight nipples. He could feel all of her—

Eric scooped her into his arms as he kept kissing her. Taking her. Claiming her with his mouth and wanting so much more.

Her legs wrapped around him. His hands gripped her hips and his cock shoved against her—long and hard and thick. Her shirt—*his* shirt—had ridden up, and his eager dick pushed right against the juncture of her thighs. He should slow down. Slow way the hell down.

But Eric felt like they were going one hundred miles an hour. He kept kissing her. Stroking her with his mouth and tongue.

She'd been great when they kissed before. Now, she was absolutely amazing, and he truly wanted to kick the asses of all the guys she'd kissed since him.

Wasted time. So much wasted time. I should have been with her.

He carried her to the table. Sat her down. Tore his hands from her hips and slammed them against the table, placing them on either side of her body even as he kept kissing her. He'd been deprived of her taste for too long. Never again. There would be no more holding back. No more trying to do what was right. She was right. They were right. Together, they were going to be—

A phone was ringing. Somewhere in the damn house, a phone was ringing.

He ignored it.

But Piper's hands flew up. She shoved against him. "I…think that's my phone." Her breath panted out.

"Let it ring." He kissed her neck. She shivered against him. Arched. He sucked her skin, right over her racing pulse.

"But…oh, jeez, that feels *good*."

He didn't hear the ringing any longer. Good. Whoever it was could just call back at a way better time.

"It's…after midnight. Why would someone call me at—"

Another peal of sound filled the air. Only this time, the peal came through on *his* phone. The one that he still had in his back pocket. He'd forgotten about the thing.

"Answer it," Piper urged.

He looked at her. Red lips. Gorgeous eyes. Flushed cheeks.

He'd done that. He'd turned her on. She felt the same savage need that he did.

Just a kiss. No, not just a kiss. A start.

The phone rang again, and, dammit, he knew that irritating ring tone. Ben. Eric backed away, breathing hard, and he yanked the phone from his pocket. "This had better be really fucking urgent," Eric began, snarling.

"It's Piper!" Ben threw right back. "I tried to get her on her phone, but she didn't answer. She's there, with you, right? She's safe?"

She was on his kitchen table looking like the best sin he'd ever seen. "She's safe. I have her." *I have her.*

"Look, I just got a call from the PD. They said they'd tried to reach her, but couldn't get through, and since I'm the contact person she has listed, they called me."

Tension swept through Eric. "What happened?"

"Her place, man—dammit!" Ben's voice was shaking. "It got torched! The uniform who was patrolling the neighborhood called it in. Some bastard set Piper's house on fire!"

CHAPTER FIVE

It could have been worse.

Piper stood on the edge of her yard, her gaze directed at her home. The sun was just starting to rise, and the sky seemed oddly red. Angry.

It could have been worse.

Yellow tape blocked the entrance, dipping across her porch. She'd expected to come back and find ashes. To have the whole place gutted.

But the uniform who'd been patrolling had called the fire department. The fire truck had rushed to the scene. Her walls were still in place. Mostly. One window was broken and a trail of black ash and soot stained the side of her home. The front door had been smashed and—

"Are you okay, Piper?"

She turned at Ben's quiet question and forced a smile. "It's not as bad as I thought." Then she finally voiced the mantra that she'd been repeating in her head. "It could have been worse."

Eric stalked up behind Ben. "Yeah, you could have been inside. That would have been one hell of a lot worse."

Piper flinched.

"Jesus, man!" Ben grabbed Piper and pulled her into his arms. "Have some tact. You don't just say shit like that." His arms surrounded her. "You've got insurance. The house will be fixed. Everything will be fine."

He felt good. Reassuring. Normal. His touch didn't make her pulse sky rocket or make her whole body become jittery. He was Ben. Her safety net.

"I'm not giving Piper lies." Eric's voice was flat and hard. "Everything isn't fine. She's got some nut-job out there who torched her house. If she'd been home, he could have killed her."

It was hard to pull in a deep breath.

"Her car was here," Eric added darkly. "The bastard could have gone in there, thinking Piper was inside. And when she wasn't, he torched the place."

Even though Ben was hugging her, she felt ice cold.

"Okay, jeez, enough. Stop grabbing on her already." Eric tugged her out of Ben's arms. "We can't stay out here forever. I just talked to the arson investigator." He pointed to a guy wearing white gloves who stood near a pick-up truck. "He told me the fire originated in your bedroom. An accelerant was definitely used, he could see the burn patterns so he knows that the perp poured the accelerant all around the room."

She shivered.

Ben immediately stepped toward her.

But before Ben could touch her again, Eric pulled her against him, wrapping his arm around her. "I've got her, okay?" Eric frowned down at her. "It's only a house. It's just things inside. What matters most is you. You're okay, and I'm going to keep you that way."

She was shivering, and, yes, the tremors were due to the cold. It was helluva cold in Atlanta that morning. Forecasters were even saying snow might come next week. But her shivers were also due to fear. Bone-deep fear. "He set my house on fire."

Eric pulled her closer. "I know, baby."

"Did you just call her 'baby'?" Ben demanded, voice rising a bit. "What the hell—"

"She's having a fucking tough day. Back off." Eric didn't even glance his way. His focus stayed on Piper. "There isn't anything you can do here now. The arson investigator has to check the entire scene. All of the hot spots inside have been put out. The fire won't start again. But you're not going to be heading in there anytime soon."

Her home. She'd bought it herself. Been so excited when she'd signed the mortgage papers. "Ben helped me paint the kitchen." They'd laughed and ordered pizza. "And we knocked down the wall between the den and the dining room because I wanted an, um, open concept." Just like she'd seen on TV.

"Nearly killed ourselves doing it," Ben added dryly.

"It was *my* home." The fear was there, but anger was growing inside of her. "He torched my home." A stranger that she didn't know. Some kind of menace in the dark.

"The uniform who saw the fire didn't get a look at the arsonist." Eric's face was tense. "The cops are going to canvass the neighborhood, but I'll have my team talk to folks, too. I also want to pull footage from the local traffic cams. The fire was set close to midnight, and there shouldn't have been many people out then. If we can find the guy on the footage, if we can get a tag number or a vehicle, we'll take him down."

She frowned at him. "You can get access to traffic cams?"

Ben sidled closer. "Legally, no, he can't." His voice was low. "But you know my big bro and his tech." A rough laugh. "Besides, Eric has always thought most rules don't apply to him."

Eric didn't look at his brother. He did give Piper a slow smile. "I'd break all of the rules if it meant keeping you safe."

That was...not nice or sweet. It probably should have been alarming. And maybe he was bullshitting, but he looked so sincere. And the way he was staring at her—

She had a flash of their kiss. Of the way she'd lost control and just wanted him.

"Why are you staring at her that way?" Ben's voice turned suspicious. "I mean, you're always intense, but you seem a little...*extra* today, bro."

Eric finally glanced at his brother. "Someone is after Piper. Hell, yes, I'm *extra*."

Sheepishly, Ben nodded. "Right." His fingers slid down Piper's arm, and he gave her a squeeze. "You're family. No one messes with our family."

But... "I'm not." She bit her lower lip. "That's what Eric reminded me last night. I'm not family."

Ben's jaw — very similar to Eric's — tightened. "The hell you aren't." He glared at Eric. "Why would you say that shit to her? You know I've never been closer to anyone than I am to her—"

"Piper isn't my family." Eric's words were growled. "But you can bet I'll protect her as if she is." He inclined his head toward his waiting Benz. "I want to take you to my office, Piper. Get you started talking with my team. Attacks like this...they aren't random. He didn't just see you on the street and decide to ruin your life."

Her stomach clenched.

"It's possible you know him." Eric shook his head. "No, not possible. You do *know* him. There are two options for that. One, he's in your life, maybe a primary player like an ex-lover or co-worker, someone who was set off when you rejected him."

That was a terrible option.

"Or, two, he's on the periphery of your world—someone who wants more attention. Either way, in most cases like this, he's connected to you, and we have to find that connection."

She needed to do *something*. Not just stand in the street and stare at the blackened side of her house. "I-I need to call my insurance agent—"

"We'll take care it," Eric assured her. His gaze slid around the street. A few of her neighbors were out, watching. "Let's go."

Ben moved into her path. "I've got a court hearing with a client at nine." He glanced at his watch, then back up at Piper. "But I'll be free the rest of the day. I'll come to you as soon as I'm done. We can get you settled for tonight. With your home like this, you're definitely going to need a longer-term housing situation."

Yes, she would. Because the repairs wouldn't magically be finished in a day or two.

"She's staying at my place. It's already taken care of." Eric's gaze was still raking the scene. "I'm having clothes and essentials brought in for her today. By the time we're done with my team, everything will be waiting for her at home."

Her brows rose. "You're getting me clothes?" Since when? "No, thanks, I can take care of my own stuff." *Arrogant much.*

"Piper," Eric sighed her name. "I told you last night that I was going to take care of things for you. Most of your clothes were slashed. Those that weren't slashed, I'm sorry but they're probably covered in ash, if they weren't burned."

He had mentioned taking care of things last night, but she hadn't been fully processing things, and she hadn't realized the guy meant he was going on a shopping spree for her. "I'll talk to your team, and then I'll go pick up supplies that I need." Luckily, her car hadn't been caught in the fire. There was some ash on the side, but otherwise, the vehicle appeared fine. She pulled away from Ben, dug into her purse, and closed her fingers around the keys. "I'll meet you at your office." She gave both Ben and Eric brisk nods before she turned and headed for her car.

Eric's crew had taken the car away on a tow truck during the night — after the fire-fighters had put out the blaze. They'd checked the vehicle and given it the all clear before bringing it back to the scene.

The little red convertible waited in her driveway, black marking its side.

At least she still had her car. It was good to go. She had her car. She had her life. She had her business.

The bastard out there — he *wasn't* going to destroy her. She wouldn't let him.

***

"Want to tell me what in the hell is going on?" Ben demanded as Piper climbed into her convertible. The top was up, so Piper was concealed when she slid inside.

Eric spared his brother a fast glance. "I'm *going* to hunt the man who did this." He wouldn't sugar coat with Ben. "This is bad, Ben. Fucking worse than I can say. I've worked cases—shit, this level of fury doesn't usually manifest so quickly."

Ben's fierce expression wavered.

"He torched her home. He *came* to this place with the accelerant. If she'd been there…" Eric didn't want to think of it. "I'm putting a guard on her. I don't want her going *anywhere* without someone watching her."

Ben retreated a step. "That's why you want her at your house? To watch her?" But he nodded before Eric could reply. "Makes sense. God, I didn't…" He rubbed a hand over his jaw. "How can I help? What can I do?"

Get out of my way, Ben. I need to follow her, now. "Call me when you're done at court. You know Piper better than anyone else." A truth that annoyed him.

And gutted him.

Ben just nodded. "Yes."

"You can tell me about her other friends. Her lovers." *Assholes I might need to take down.* "Anyone who might have a personal grudge against her."

His brother seemed confused. "She can tell you all of that stuff."

"It helps to get another perspective. In cases like this, sometimes, the victims can't see what's right in front of them. They don't realize the danger because it's hidden behind a friendly face." A friendly face could be the most dangerous one in the entire world.

Ben's lips pressed together. Then, as if considering, he said, "Everyone always loves Piper. At least, that's the way it seems."

Someone might love her too much.

She was backing out of the drive. "I'm going behind her. Call me when you're done with court." He turned for his vehicle.

"It's...nice of you to help her out this way. I appreciate it. I owe you."

Nice? Eric's shoulders stiffened. "You don't owe me anything." He fired a fast glance back at his brother. "I'm not doing this for you. It's for Piper."

A half-smile curved Ben's lips. "Finally gave in to her charm, huh? Like I said...everyone always loves Piper."

***

She'd been to Wilde Securities before. More than a dozen times. The tall, dominating building sat in the heart of downtown Atlanta. And Eric's office—the big corner office on the top floor—offered a killer view of the city.

"Do you want something to drink?" Eric's assistant gave her a quick, nervous smile before he pushed up the frame of his glasses. Dennis had a friendly, open face. Just out of college last spring, Dennis was a newer hire, one who seemed very eager to make his way at Wilde Securities.

"I'm good, thanks." She slid onto the nearby couch. Eric wasn't in the office. He'd escorted her in, then done a quick disappearing act. But he'd asked her to wait there for him.

Her hands twisted in her lap. She wasn't particularly good at waiting, especially when she kept thinking about her house. The fire. And whoever the hell had set it.

"I'll be right outside." Dennis nodded. "If you need me, just call."

"Thank you, I—"

The door opened behind Dennis. "Piper!" Simon Forrest's booming voice filled the room as he rushed toward her. "Eric told me about the fire!"

She jumped to her feet, right before Simon hauled her in for a bone-crushing hug. He was as big as Eric, just as tall and as broad in the shoulders. The first time she'd met Simon, he'd asked her out.

Considering that the guy looked like some sort of Viking God...uh, specifically, her favorite, Thor, she'd been way inclined to say yes to him. A dark-haired Thor was pretty awesome.

But then Eric had destroyed those plans. He'd told her that Simon was too dangerous, that the guy lived for adrenaline. An ex-SEAL, Simon wasn't exactly a safe guy.

Since she hadn't ever been particularly attracted to safe, Piper had still been ready to give Simon and his date a try, but then Eric had spoken privately with his new VP. And Simon had suddenly gone very, very cold on her.

He didn't feel cold right then.

He gave her another squeeze. "You'll be taken care of." His breath blew over her ear. "Wilde Securities is on the job."

"Get your hands off her!" Eric's snarling — and pissed — voice.

Simon pulled back. His hands lingered on her shoulders. "You okay?"

Piper nodded.

"Still touching her. Stop that shit." Eric had stalked inside the office. Again, the man must have used his sneaky ninja skills because she hadn't heard him enter the room, yet he now stood behind his massive desk, glowering at them.

Simon stopped 'that shit.' He let her go. Moved back.

"Dennis, hold my calls, will you?" Eric growled at his assistant.

She'd forgotten Dennis was still there.

Dennis nodded as he hurriedly exited the room. The door shut behind him with a soft click.

And Piper twisted her hands again.

Eric's glower got a little worse. "You're safe."

"Absolutely," Simon added with his big, tiger smile.

"I don't feel safe." Far from it. Instead of taking a seat on the couch again, she paced toward the floor to ceiling windows that faced the city. The work day had started, and the cars were rushing on the street below. "When are you going to be able to access the traffic cams, Eric?"

"Already got techs working on them now." Eric's leather chair gave a soft groan as he sat down. "As soon as they have something, they'll report to me immediately."

That was good.

"And we have investigators with arson experience," Eric added as the leather groaned again. "I've sent Julia Slate and Rick Williams over to your house, Piper. They're both former firefighters, and they'll make sure no detail is overlooked there."

Okay. So, action was happening. Things were moving. She rolled back her shoulders. Straightened her spine. "What can I do?"

Silence.

She turned toward the men, her gaze sliding first to Eric. He stared back at her, and, God, had they really been kissing just hours before? A kiss that had nearly knocked her right off her feet. Eric Wilde. The kiss had been even better than the one they'd shared so many years ago. And was it possible...had he really wanted her way back then? *Did* he still want her?

As she stared into his eyes, she could have sworn that she saw need. Longing. For her?

But...it was Eric. *Eric.*

If the call hadn't interrupted them, what would have happened?

What would happen if she stayed at his place again the coming night?

Her cheeks burned as she yanked her stare away from him and peered over at Simon. He was frowning. Staring suspiciously at her...and Eric.

"We need to know the people who are close to you," Simon finally said. He pulled a small laptop from his bag. She hadn't even noticed the bag until that moment. He'd had the satchel slung over one shoulder. "Let's make a list because that's going to be our starting point."

She took one step toward him. "You really think the person doing this is someone I know?"

"Odds are good that he is," Eric replied in his deep, dark voice. "Crimes like this aren't usually random."

"But they *can* be random?" It couldn't be someone she knew. This—everything that had happened—there was so much rage. Rage meant hate, didn't it? Who could hate her this much?

"It can be random," Simon allowed with his fingers curled around the laptop, "but we're going to be smart about this. We're going to investigate the people close to you and then work our way outward. It's the way Eric always operates in these situations."

These situations. She risked another glance Eric's way. "You do so much more than just design security systems for homes and businesses."

Eric inclined his head toward her. "Personal protection was the logical, next step in my business plan. I wanted to offer a total package to clients."

"You've...stopped other guys like this?"

He reached for a pen on his desk. His fingers balled around it. "Yes. And we will stop this one, too."

He said the words with such certainty that some of the tension eased from her shoulders. "Thank you."

He gave her a small smile. "But we need the list, Piper. I get that it's personal, but we need to know everyone who is close to you." He waved to the chair in front of his desk. "Why don't you take a seat and we'll get started?"

Okay. *Let's do this.* She eased into the chair. Her sneakers slid over the floor. "Ben." It felt crazy just to say his name. "I mean, obviously, he's not the one doing this. But he's the person closest to me. The one who knows all of my deep, dark secrets."

Simon settled into the chair next to her. He put his laptop on Eric's desk. "Do you have a lot of those secrets?"

She laughed, then realized he wasn't kidding.

"Because dark secrets can attract dark people," Simon added. "If you've got something in your past that you've buried deep, this is the time to tell us."

He was dead serious. "There's nothing." Her head turned toward Eric. "There isn't!"

"We are going to have to investigate your life, as part of this case." Simon's voice was very careful. "It's just easier if we start by knowing the secrets instead of having to uncover them and question you more later. Saves us time, you understand?"

She couldn't read the expression in Eric's eyes. "You've known me most of my life. I don't have dark secrets."

"We all have them," Simon told her. "Eric sure has plenty."

"Watch it," Eric rasped at him.

"Watching it." Simon cleared his throat. "Moving on…current lover."

He wanted to know her current lover? Easy. "I…don't have one."

He nodded. "Okay, then let's start with your most recent lover and work our way back from there. You can just tell me when Ben fits into this mix." The last was said as an off-hand aside. Like it was a given.

And it pissed her off. "Seriously?" Her voice rose to an alarming degree. "Why does everyone think I've slept with Ben?"

Simon looked over at her and blinked. Then he shook his head. "I am so sorry. Look, I don't mean to make you feel uncomfortable. We want you to talk freely with us. We want to help. I just thought by mentioning Ben—I mean, you just said he was the person closest to you—I figured it would be easier—"

She held up her hand. "Stop." Piper pulled in a deep breath. "There's a big misconception here. Obviously, one that you and Eric both share. Let's just start with this, okay? I have not ever been Ben's lover."

Simon frowned. He typed something on his laptop.

She directed her attention to Eric. "Is that point well covered now?"

A muscle jerked in his jaw. "Very well, thank you."

"As for other lovers, I mean...I just don't think they'd do this. My last lover—Zane Clarke—our relationship ended a year ago. It wasn't the best end, but it wasn't some nightmare, either."

Simon was typing. She could hear the faint click of the keys, but she couldn't seem to drag her gaze off Eric.

"Why did it end?" Eric asked quietly.

"He got a job in Chicago. He wanted me to move with him." She lifted one shoulder in a shrug. "I didn't want to go." Because she hadn't loved him. "So, we went our separate ways."

Eric held her gaze. "Before him?"

"Before him I was involved with Grady Fox." And she smiled saying his name. Fun, easy-going Grady.

"That was in college."

She lifted an eyebrow at Eric's words. "Yes."

"You…you…" He kind of sputtered away. "How many lovers have you had?"

She leaned forward, putting her palms on the desk. "This is truly one of the most awkward conversations I've had in ages. Since it is so awkward, I think you're going to owe me. Tit for tat. I want to know how many lovers you've had, Eric."

He blinked at her.

"No? Maybe later? I think later, yes." She sighed. Her fingers tapped on his desk. "Two. I've had two lovers because I don't just sleep with anyone, all right? You know I am *super* picky with my food. Did you think I'd be different with my lovers?"

Eric's face seemed to have been carved from absolute stone. But his eyes sure were dark. Even darker than normal.

"Next question?" Piper pushed as she glanced at Simon. "Can we have the next question, please?"

Simon coughed. "If not lovers, then how about guys you've dated? I'll need a list of those individuals."

"Sure." Dating was fun. She liked getting to know people. Liked dancing and dining out. But if there wasn't a connection, she didn't go past the dating stage.

I sure felt a connection with Eric last night. Despite the madness in her life, she'd felt a connection that had left her knees shaking.

"I should get a list of your employees, too," Simon mused. "Everyone at your gallery. Friends, then casual acquaintances as we broaden the circle around you."

Her temples were throbbing. "This is going to take forever."

Simon just nodded.

So she got started. "Fine, the last guy I dated was Mark Rogue." Piper glanced over at the laptop. "He owns a tattoo shop close to the gallery. It's called Go Rogue."

"Is that how you met?" Simon asked, not looking up. "You ran into him one day on your way to the gallery?"

For the first time that day, she laughed, the warm sound slipping out of her. "Of course, not. I met Mark when I got my tattoo."

"Fuck me."

Her gaze snapped to Eric. "Excuse me?"

Eric rubbed his eyes. And clenched his jaw. "Where is the tattoo?"

"It's on my ankle. Can't believe you haven't seen it. Guess you just don't pay enough attention to me."

"*Piper.*"

"It's a small half moon. I got it when I opened my gallery. My gallery *is* called Moonlight, and opening it was the most important thing I've done. I wanted something to remember the moment by, so I got the tat." She smiled. Then got back to business. "Before Mark, I dated Carmen Bright. He's a boxer down at White's Gym."

Simon's head snapped toward her. "He's in line for the championship fight."

Yes, he was.

"Then there was Tony Lovett. Great cook." He had a restaurant in Atlanta that was booming and a new cable TV cooking show. She tapped her chin. "Before him, let me see..."

Eric growled.

She narrowed her eyes at him. "There a problem?" She'd never realized he growled so much. It was weird.

He exhaled slowly. "I gave that bastard money to start his restaurant."

Piper nodded. "Yes, Tony told me. That was really nice of you."

"He *never* mentioned you. Ben brought him to me, wanted us to go in as silent partners backing the guy..." He swallowed. "Was part of that *your* idea?"

Ah...*tread carefully*. "Ben mentioned that you wanted to diversify a bit. Backing Tony seemed like a good business plan."

"Sonofabitch."

Simon had gone dead quiet.

Eric rolled his shoulders. "Something to remember, Piper, I'm not *nice*." A smile came across his face, one that was ice cold. "Especially when people try to hurt the things that belong to *me*."

The way he was staring at her, so intense, so determined…it was almost as if…No, no way.

He didn't think that she belonged to him. Impossible.

"When someone tries to take something that is mine, I retaliate. Fucking lethal retaliation."

CHAPTER SIX

"Okay, I got here as fast as I could." Ben blew out a hard breath. "Court case ran long. The fight is vicious. My client *hates* her husband. I swear, I am never getting married."

Eric glared at his brother. The asshole had been keeping secrets.

Ben winced. "Sorry, okay?" A pause that lasted only a beat. "Where's Piper?"

"She's with Simon. He had a few more questions for her." Just as Eric had some questions for his brother.

Ben dropped into the chair across from Eric's desk. "Any leads? Do we know anything new?"

Something new? Yes. He knew that Piper had only been with two lovers. He knew she had a tattoo. One he'd love to see. But did he know who was terrorizing her? Hell, the fuck, *no*. "Piper sees the world through rose-colored glasses. When she talks about her past relationships, she says they all ended amicably. No problems. No big drama."

Ben's shoulders slouched a bit. He rubbed the tip of his nose.

"You're the best divorce attorney in Atlanta," Eric said, not stroking his brother's ego, but just being honest. Ben had completed an accelerated Juris Doctor program at Georgia State so that he'd wound up finishing his undergraduate *and* law degree work in six years. As soon as he'd started practicing, the guy immediately dominated the courtroom. "And we both know that not every relationship ends *well*."

Ben's lashes shielded his gaze.

"I want your take. You think any of her exes could do this? You think there is someone I should be focused on right now?"

"Piper doesn't...she doesn't get serious." Ben seemed to be carefully considering his words. "You know what it was like when her dad cut out on her mom all those years ago. Her mother, Jesus, she was shattered. Drank herself to death after he left. No matter what Piper did, she couldn't get her mom to stop grabbing for the bottle. She couldn't get her mom to see there was still a life worth living."

Beneath his desk, Eric's hands clenched. Piper's dad had left her family when she was fourteen. He'd run off with a younger woman. Divorced Piper's mom. Started a new life somewhere. As far as Eric knew, Piper hadn't seen or talked to her dad in years. As for her mom...

Her mom had died in a drunk driving accident during Piper's second year of college.

Eric had gone to the funeral. Ben had been at Piper's right side. And Eric had been at her left. He'd taken her hand, and he'd just held her. She hadn't cried, but her expression had broken his heart.

I knew I was in trouble back then. Maybe I always knew.

"After her mom died, that was when she broke it off with that Grady guy, too. They got into some kind of fight just a few days after she buried her mom. I think it was because the jerk didn't show up for her mom's funeral. He was on some kind of fraternity trip, instead. She needed him, and he wasn't there. Piper..." His stare locked on Eric. "She doesn't trust easily. She doesn't believe in forever. She lives in the moment. She doesn't want commitment because she doesn't think it lasts. To her, there *is* no relationship that will last forever."

So many things were clicking into place now. "Except her relationship with you."

Ben nodded. "Because I don't want anything from her. Never have. That's the thing about best friends, you know? I am her constant, and I always will be."

Eric surged to his feet. "We had to ask Piper for a list of her lovers so we could investigate them." He paced toward the window. "You weren't on the list."

Ben gave a quick bark of laughter. "Uh, yeah, no big surprise."

Sonofa—He spun to face his brother. "I heard you, back in high school, tell Clarence Wells that she was your first."

Ben gaped at him. "What?" Then his eyes widened. "Dumbass!" Ben jumped to his feet. "You didn't tell Piper that shit, did you?"

Well…

"Dammit!" Ben jerked back his head. "What the actual fuck? I was just mouthing off! The jerk was giving me a hard time because I was a virgin. I was a teenage punk who just said something stupid." He rocked back on his heels. "Piper is going to kill me. I will need to grovel at her feet for weeks. Buy her a truck load of her chocolate chip cookie dough ice cream."

"You shouldn't have lied," Eric gritted out.

"I lied for a day! And I was just a stupid kid! I felt like shit about the lie so I went back to Clarence the next morning and told him the truth!" He ran a hand over his face. "The asshat called me 'Ben the Virgin' for weeks after that. But I wasn't going to let people start spreading rumors about Piper. I got my shit together and told the truth because no one has ever mattered to me more than she does." Now he closed the distance between them. Stood toe-to-toe with Eric. "That's why I'm asking you right now— what the hell is going on? Why are you doing all of this for her?"

"Because she matters to me, too. She's been in my life just as long as she's been in yours." That was all he'd tell his brother. Because what was happening between him and Piper—she'd asked that he not say anything to Ben.

Did the woman realize he'd do *anything* for her?

Ben sucked in a deep breath. "They didn't all end well."

Eric frowned.

"Some of those guys wanted more from her. More than she was willing to give them. They didn't know about her past. They didn't know why she shut them down so fast when they started pushing for a commitment. They wanted more. Some of them were pissed when they didn't get it."

Anger flared within him. "I'll need those names."

Ben backed up. "Yeah, I thought you would…Grady Fox? You're gonna want to put him at the top of the list."

***

"You didn't have to come shopping with me." Piper glanced at the bags Eric was carrying out of the store. "I mean, I know you have work to do. A company to run. And I'm a big girl. I'm used to shopping on my own."

Yeah, of course, he knew she could shop on her own, but he wanted her *safe*. To him, safety meant she stayed close to him. He hit a button on his key fob and the Benz's trunk popped open. He dropped the bags inside, and the small, pink bag with the discreet lingerie logo slid to the side.

Fuck, fuck, fuck. He eyed the small bit of white lace—

Piper shoved the lace back into the bag. "And you definitely didn't need to *pay* for my things. I have my own money. I certainly don't need you—"

"It would be great if you did." The words just rolled out of him. Dammit, wrong thing to say.

She frowned. The cute, from the corner of her eye frown that she always gave him. "I don't understand."

He slammed the trunk, took her hand, and walked her around to the passenger side of the car. But he didn't open the door. For a moment, he just stood there, staring into her beautiful eyes. Gold was his favorite color. "I'd like for you to need me."

He heard the swift inhalation of her breath. "Eric…"

This time, he smiled. "I like the way you say my name. When you're nervous, your voice rises with it. When you're mad, you barely breathe it, and when you're happy…" He caught a lock of hair and tucked it behind her ear. "You almost moan it."

Her golden eyes widened. "I do not."

He shrugged. "Consider the clothes a gift. And there is no repaying a gift."

She searched his gaze. "Why are you here?"

"Because you need a guard with you until we find out what's happening." And as far as *what* his team was doing…Simon had already started all of the standard background checks on the people she'd listed during her interview. "If anything pops during the background run, if we see any red flags, I'll be told immediately."

Piper nibbled on her lower lip. That sexy, full lip.

Did she want him to beg?

She let her lip go. "I'm sure there's a junior agent who can be my guard. You have other things to do. I don't expect you to — to give me like the deluxe, white glove treatment or anything."

He leaned closer to her, putting his hand on the top of the car and caging her there with his body. "I don't usually work bodyguard cases, but you aren't a routine case." He needed to stay close to her. When he'd seen the fire at her place…

Dammit.

He should back away. Get in the car. Stop inhaling her sweet scent and remembering how good she'd tasted.

He'd been craving ice cream all day long.

"Eric?"

"You said you wanted to go to your gallery." A brisk nod. "I want to check out the place, too. See what additions I can make to the security there." *And while I'm at the gallery, I can walk down the street, maybe check out the tattoo artist.* "We'll stop there next."

"That's awfully nice of you."

A soft rumble of laughter escaped him. "I think we've covered that I'm not the nice one. That's Ben, remember?"

A car horn sounded in the distance, and his head whipped to the left. They were inside a cavernous parking garage, and a blue SUV had just slid around the corner.

They needed to get moving. He backed away, opened her door, and waited until she slid inside. A few moments later, he was in the driver's seat and reversing the vehicle.

"I-I think you are being nice." Her voice was halting. "And you've…been nice to me a few other times over the years."

He'd also been a dick over the years. His hold tightened on the steering wheel. "I should have always been better to you. It's time things change."

Her scent came to him again as they drove. Did she have any idea how much he loved her lavender scent? How much he—

"I need to pay for your services."

He braked at a red light. "What?"

"Your protection. I need to pay for it."

Eric slanted her a glance, but she just looked so damn innocent. "You're not paying me, Piper."

"Oh, yes, I am."

"No, you're not. I'm helping you because security is my business."

"But you don't run a charity business! Look, it's bad enough you wouldn't let me pay when you installed the initial security system at my gallery."

And he sure as hell wished he'd been the one to install the system at her home, too. But they'd gotten into a fight at her gallery that day…because he'd been a jealous dumbass. Some idiot artist had come in, calling her his muse, going on and on about how she'd inspired him…

Eric was pretty sure he'd told the fellow to fuck off because they were busy.

Piper hadn't liked that response very much. After he'd finished the install, she'd kicked him out. Eric didn't know what had happened with the dumbass artist. What had his name been? Dillon? Dante? He'd have to check with Simon to make sure the fellow was on their investigation list.

A car honked behind him. He wondered how long the light had been green. Eric shoved down on the gas, and the Benz surged forward. "It's not charity to help a friend."

"Is that what I am?"

Another red light. He braked. Turned toward her. "What do you want to be?"

Her golden eyes were so deep.

"That's the real question, Piper. What do you want? Do you want to be my *friend?* The way you are friends with Ben? Or do you want to be something more? Because I'm telling you right now, I want more."

The light changed. He didn't wait for a honk. He just drove straight ahead. Piper hadn't answered him. Not yet. They drove in silence the rest of the way to her gallery, and when he pulled into the open space right in front of her building, he was still trying to figure out exactly what he should say to her.

After killing the engine, Eric turned to her. He needed to tell her something reassuring. Something charming and easy. But when he opened his mouth—"Why only two lovers?" *Those* words burst out.

A small furrow appeared between her brows. "Two what?"

"Lovers. You only had two lovers. Why only two?"

"Because..." She leaned closer to him, as if she was about to impart a massive secret. "I don't let just anyone into my vagina."

God, she had not—she'd just—

Piper smiled at him. Then she laughed. "Your face is priceless."

Her laughter was sweet and soft.

"*I* choose my lovers, Eric, and I choose carefully. I need to feel a connection, a white-hot intensity, and if that's not there, then I don't want to waste my—"

He kissed her. Because her smile was beautiful. Because her laugh was the best music he'd ever heard. Because he craved her, not ice cream. And as soon as his lips touched hers, the explosion of need erupted again.

He'd been trying for a tender kiss. A careful brush of his lips against hers. Instead, he kissed her once, softly, lifted his lips, and then he went back for more. His hands rose and sank into her hair as he kissed her with a wild ferocity. A stark lust.

She gave a little moan in the back of her throat. And she kissed him back the same way. With primitive, desperate desire. With a sensual need that shook him to his core. With a fierce hunger that made him ache.

His heartbeat thundered in his ears as he forced his head to lift. "Is it there?" *A white-hot intensity.*

Her breath came fast. Her eyes had darkened. "Yes."

"Then what are we going to do about it?"

She turned away. Fumbled with the door. Forced it open and climbed from the car. Swearing, he hurried to follow her. Eric caught her wrist in his hand. "Piper—" He surged closer to her.

"Everything will change." She stared up at him. Fear flickered in her eyes. "What happens then?"

Anything we want.

But he needed to back off. Piper was right. Everything was *her* choice. So, he sucked in a breath, and he let her go.

While she unlocked the door to her gallery, he scanned the street. He didn't see any sign of Piper's stalker, but the guy could be very good at hiding. It was late on a Friday evening, and the sky was already starting to darken. It would be easy for someone to hide in the darkness.

The bell over her shop gave a cheery ring as Piper slipped inside, and he entered right behind her, watching as Piper reset the alarm.

"I had already scheduled for the gallery to be closed today." She put her keys on the counter. "I'd been out of town on a scouting trip before…" Her hand waved vaguely in the air.

"Before you came back and found your home trashed?"

A quick nod. "I'd intended to do some re-organizing in here next week. I gave my assistant last week off while I traveled. We were planning to start fresh Monday." She let her hand fall. "Everything looks okay in here."

Her gallery. For as long as he could remember, Piper had loved painting. When she'd been a kid, her shorts and t-shirts had always been covered with paint splotches. He'd thought it was funny, just kind of a Piper thing, until he'd actually seen her work.

Piper wasn't just a good artist. She was phenomenal. Even at twelve, she'd painted things that—damn, he didn't always have words for them. The woman had simply been born with a gift. She could make emotion explode off a canvas.

She'd just gotten better and better as she aged. And the gallery—hell, she didn't *need* the place. But it had been her brainchild. Her work had been selling like crazy, and she'd started to get some national attention. She'd come up with the idea of opening a gallery to spotlight other artists, too. Emerging talent.

At least, that was what she'd told Ben. Because she hadn't come to Eric with her plans.

Maybe one day, that would change.

She usually kept the gallery open three days a week. The other four days, she worked on her art. She held big shows two to three times a month at her gallery, and he knew that they were always hits. He'd come to a few. Drank the champagne she offered. Watched her charm and impress.

That was Piper.

Everyone always loves Piper. Yeah, they sure as hell did.

"I want to go and check upstairs. I've got some of my new work up there, and I want to make sure it's all okay. Give me a minute, will you?"

Her studio was upstairs—so that she could look out on the street below. So she could see the sunrise and sunsets. He knew she could get lost in her work.

He could, too. He could stare at her work for hours because he *felt* Piper in those canvases. She put all of herself into the art.

She hurried up the small, spiral staircase. Her steps echoed when they thudded over the metal stairs. Faint light from the setting sun drifted through the upper windows. He kept his gaze on her as she neared the second floor—her loft area. Her work area, her—

She disappeared, just for a second when she left the stairs. He waited for her to reappear.

"Eric!"

There was fear and anger in her voice, and he immediately bounded up the stairs after her. He grabbed the metal railing and rushed up, his heart racing, and when he cleared the top, sonofabitch, there was blood everywhere.

Every-fucking-where.

CHAPTER SEVEN

The truth sank in with his second, frantic glance. No, it wasn't blood. It was paint. Red paint had been poured all over her floor. Thrown onto the walls. Thrown onto the canvases.

Shit. The canvases.

Piper stood—statue-still—in front of a large canvas. The red paint had dried in streaks on it. "I was almost finished with this piece. It...it was for a show I'm doing next month." Jerkily, her head moved as she looked at the other canvases that had been covered in red paint. "They were for the show. I've lost them all."

Rage poured through him.

Her hand lifted, as if she'd touch her canvas.

He rushed to her, catching her fingers in his. "Don't touch anything, baby. I want my team out here."

She blinked. "The alarm didn't go off." Her lower lip trembled. "After the break-in at my house, I came here. I looked downstairs. Everything was fine there, so I didn't even think to come up here and look around. I didn't know."

Tears filled her eyes. "He torched my home. He destroyed my work. He—"

Eric pulled her into his arms, pulled her against his chest, and wrapped her in his embrace. He held her tightly and wished that he could take away every single bit of her pain.

Even as he wanted to destroy the sonofabitch who'd done this to her.

"What is he going to do next?" Piper whispered. "What will he do to me next?"

"Nothing," Eric promised her. "I'm not going to let him. I swear it." The security system there was his. He'd find out why the hell it hadn't sent out an alert. He'd review all of the camera footage and motion sensor data. He'd find out when the bastard had come to her place.

Then he'd get local traffic cam videos. He'd *nail* the piece of shit.

"We need to get out of here, Piper." He was still holding her in his arms. "We don't want to destroy any evidence left behind. I'll have my team here within the next five minutes."

"We should call the cops."

Yeah, he would. But he wanted his team on scene first.

He stared down at her. Hated the tear that had slid down her cheek. His hand rose, and he brushed it away, his fingers lingering against her silken skin. "I will make this better." A promise that went soul-deep. And the first way to make it better? Get her out of there. Take her to safety.

"Come on, Piper." He twined his fingers with hers and led the way downstairs. Every muscle in his body was tight with fury and tension. Piper had been hurt, again, by this bastard. That shit wasn't going to keep happening. Not on his watch.

Before he took her out of the gallery, he texted his team. Eric knew he'd get an immediate response. They exited the building, he secured the door behind them, and his gaze swept the area as he looked for any potential threats.

And, sure-the-hell-enough, he saw a shadowy figure moving toward them. Eric pushed Piper behind him, shielding her with his body as the figure came closer. A guy, tall, with a quick pace and wearing a hoodie—

"Piper!" The shout came from the guy as he finally cleared the shadows. "Thought I saw lights in your place." He took another step toward them. No, toward Piper.

"Stay the fuck back," Eric snarled.

The man blinked and shoved back his hood, revealing bright, blond hair. "Uh, Piper? Everything okay?" His head cocked as he tried to see her body behind Eric. "This guy giving you trouble?" And his voice went rougher.

Eric's gaze raked him. The man had tousled hair, a pretty-boy face, and he wore a thick hoodie and jeans. But near his wrists, when the fabric of the hoodie sweatshirt slid back, Eric could just make out the dark etchings of tattoos. There were tattoos sliding up his neck, too. Black, twisting lines.

The man had been close by...close enough to see lights in the gallery.

Figured the fellow must be—

"Mark," Piper's voice drifted in the growing darkness. "Someone broke into my gallery. Destroyed my work. We're calling the police."

Mark Rogue's face hardened. "Seriously? Shit!" And he hurried forward, reaching out his hands—

Eric made sure he stayed between the guy and Piper. "I think that I told you already...stay the fuck back. There isn't going to be another warning."

Mark blinked. "Uh, Piper? This the new boyfriend?"

"No," she said.

"Yes," Eric fired in the same instant. "And I don't like it when random bastards come out of the shadows and head for Piper." Especially when he'd just left the twisted mess in the gallery.

Mark's brow furrowed at their mixed responses. "Piper?"

"Eric is...a friend. And my, um, bodyguard?" The last seemed like a question.

Since she was unsure, Eric decided to help her out. "Friend, bodyguard, boyfriend. Whatever she needs me to be. Mostly, I'm the guy telling you that *no one* else is getting close to her."

Mark's hands clenched and unclenched. "Did someone really break into her place?"

"Yes," Eric snapped. "And then we walked outside, and guess who came running up?"

Mark took a step back. Finally. "I would never do anything to hurt Piper!"

Eric wasn't exactly ready to take the other man's word for it.

"Piper, dammit!" Mark exploded. "Tell him I wouldn't do this! You know me! Tell him—" And the guy surged forward. His hands were in angry fists and those fists seemed to be coming straight for Eric.

So much for *finally* getting the message to back up.

Mark lunged, Piper screamed, and Eric reacted.

He drove one hand into Mark's stomach, then plowed a powerful punch into the guy's jaw. Mark hit the ground with a thud. Eric stood over him, hands fisted, ready for another attack. "I told you…stay the fuck away from her."

Mark groaned.

"What did you do?" Piper's voice was hushed. Horrified.

In the distance, a siren screamed. Eric knew his team had alerted the cops. They'd all be reaching the scene soon.

"You just assaulted me…*asshole*," Mark gasped as he shoved to his feet. His breath heaved in and out. "You won't get another lucky shot again. You won't get—"

"Don't, Mark!" Piper yelled. "Stop this, now!" And she shoved between the two men. "Don't do this."

Her voice was shaking. *She* was shaking.

The siren grew louder.

Mark's shoulders sagged. "I would never do anything to hurt Piper." His gaze was on Eric. "I owe her too much."

"Mark…" Piper shook her head. "You don't have to—"

"I'm sober because of her. She saved my damn life. Literally took the bottle out of my hand and stopped me before I killed my dumb ass."

The siren was louder. Closer.

"You think I'd *ever* do anything to harm so much as a hair on her head?" Mark's voice was heavy with tension. "No, I wouldn't. You're dead wrong, bastard. Dead wrong."

***

She'd seen Eric fight before. He'd fought plenty of times when they were kids. Always seemed to get into scrapes. And he worked out at the local boxing ring. Heck, she'd even met her ex, Carmen, when she'd gone to meet Ben and Eric at the gym one time.

Eric's parents had started him and Ben in marital arts when they'd just been teens. Eric had loved everything he'd learned. He'd studied all the time, and he'd branched off into different styles, learning Taekwondo, karate, judo...But she knew his favorite form of defense was Krav Maga. Before she'd left for college, he'd even dragged her to classes. He'd said she had to be ready to defend herself.

So, yes, she knew Eric was strong. She knew he was fast. But he'd pounded Mark before she could so much as blink.

"The new boyfriend seems...way protective." Mark's voice was stilted as he approached her.

She stood next to Eric's car, her hips propped against the side of the vehicle. At his words, she tilted her head.

"Protective..." Mark said again. "Fucking dangerous. Take your pick."

Piper swallowed. Eric was talking to two members of his team and one of the uniformed cops who'd arrived. "He's not my boyfriend, and he's not dangerous."

"Uh, yeah, tell that to someone who isn't sporting a bruised jaw because of him."

Right. "Some...things have been happening lately. He's like—Eric is like my bodyguard, and when you lunged forward, he reacted, thinking you were attacking me."

He closed the space between them. Stared down at her. "I would never do that to you.

Would never want you hurt. I wasn't bullshitting back there. You saved my ass."

She glanced away from him, the memories stirring in her mind. She'd been taking out the trash one day, walking in the narrow alley behind her building, and she'd found him. Passed out, a broken bottle of Jack at his side. She hadn't been able to leave him because she'd remembered all the times her mother had come home and passed out on the couch…

Until the day she didn't come home.

Piper had dragged Mark, literally hauled him inch by painful inch, back to her gallery. She'd sobered him up with coffee. And she'd asked him…why.

Mark's sister had been murdered—one year to the day that Piper had found him in that alley. When he'd talked to her, when he'd told Piper his story, Mark had said it was his fault. He'd been supposed to pick up his sister after work, but he'd gotten distracted. He'd arrived an hour late.

His sister had been dead when he found her. She'd been viciously stabbed, over and over again.

Her killer had never been caught.

Piper had been able to tell by Mark's eyes…the guilt had been eating him from the inside out.

"After what happened to Katie, shit, you *know* I'd want to help you. If some bastard out there is targeting you, *talk* to me. Let me help you!"

Piper exhaled slowly. "Eric runs Wilde Securities. He's helping me. Providing around the clock protection." She pointed toward Eric. "His team is on the case."

At that moment, Eric looked up. His gaze zeroed in on her. Even in the growing darkness, she could feel the heat of his stare.

Then his head turned, and she knew he was staring at Mark. Eric said something else to the people around him, then he began marching her way.

"Someone torched my house last night," she told Mark. "And now I found out that my paintings were destroyed, too. I don't know who is doing this, but, Mark, if you saw *anything*, I mean, if you noticed anyone around my gallery, if anything suspicious stuck out at you, please tell me."

"I didn't see anyone," he told her grimly. "But I'll check all of my security feeds."

"I'd like access to the footage," Eric said as he closed in on them.

Mark cursed. "Look, buddy, I don't exactly fucking *like* you—"

"And I don't like you, so we're even, but I want that footage."

Mark nodded. "Fine. For Piper. Because I'd do anything for her."

Eric positioned his body next to her even as his stare raked over the other man. "You're in love with her."

She felt her face burn. No, Mark wasn't *in* love with her. He was grateful to her. He wanted to pay her back for what she'd done for him. But as far as romance was concerned, things between them had never really heated up. They were in the friend zone because when she looked at him, she wanted to — to help. There was no passion, no intensity, no —

"So the fuck are you," Mark threw back. "Or else you wouldn't be walking a tightrope of fear and fury. You think I can't see it? You lost your shit when I got close to her—"

"You lunged to attack. Piper screamed." A shrug. "She was scared. I can't have her scared."

"Because *you're* fucking in love with—"

"He's not in love with me," Piper cut in immediately. That was just crazy. "We're…friends. Very old friends."

Eric took her hand in his. Laced his fingers with hers. "Listen, Rogue, I told you — twice — to back off. You should have listened. If you'd listened and not attacked, I wouldn't have needed to stop you."

"And you should have told me what was going on! If I'd realized you just came from a scene where her paintings were destroyed, I would've got that you were already on the edge of a major freak out—"

"I don't think you get many things about me." His voice was flat, but then Eric glanced down at her. When he spoke again, his voice softened as he said, "Baby, we need to go. My team has this, and the cops aren't going to be leaving anytime soon. Let me take you home."

Her home had been torched.

"*My* home," he said, as if reading her thoughts. "I need to know that you're safe."

A sad laugh came from her. "Yes, I'd like to know that, too." Screw it. She was going home with him. Why fight? She wanted the safety that he could provide to her right then. She cast a quick glance at Mark. "Give him the footage as soon as you can."

"For you, anything."

She headed for her car. When his agents had come to the scene, Eric had ordered one of them to bring her car to the gallery. She was damn glad that he had — she *wanted* the freedom and control of being in her own ride. Her fingers slid over the key fob, unlocking it. Before she could reach for the door, Eric was there. He opened it for her and stood back, watching, while she slid into the seat.

"I'll be right behind you."

She stared through the windshield, gazing at her gallery. Police tape had already been rolled across the front of the building. She was in a nightmare, and things were just getting worse.

Eric slammed the door shut and strode away. Piper glanced in her rear-view mirror and saw him head back toward Mark. He said something to the guy, and she wondered what they were talking about. Eric handed Mark what looked like a business card. Mark took the card, gave a jerky nod, and stepped back.

A moment later, Eric was in his car. His lights flashed on.

A tear slid down Piper's cheek as she drove away.

This night sucked. This week sucked. The bastard doing this to her—*he sucked.*

***

Piper had found his tribute. She'd gone into her gallery and seen the work he'd done. He'd been waiting, knowing that she would go back there. Art was in Piper's soul. There was no way she could stay away. He'd just needed to get close. Needed to wait.

She drove away slowly, followed immediately by the prick in the Benz. The guy who acted as if he had some sort of right to her.

He didn't.

Piper is mine.

No one noticed when he slowly pulled onto the street and followed the Benz. Piper wasn't getting away from him. He'd find out where she was going. He'd keep a very close watch on her.

I've got you now, Piper.

She wouldn't be able to hide, not anymore.

Because wherever she went, he could find her.

He wondered what she'd thought of his tribute. Did she realize how very much she inspired him? If she didn't…

She would.

Very, very soon.

CHAPTER EIGHT

You're fucking in love with her, too.

Eric stared into the flames. The fire crackled and danced in his study, the flames moving quickly. He'd returned home and lit the fire, thinking that Piper might want to come downstairs and join him, that she might want to talk after everything that had happened.

But she'd gone straight to her room. Shut the door. Closed him out.

Shit. He'd lost his control in front of her. He hadn't meant for that to happen. But when Mark had lunged for her and Piper's terrified scream filled Eric's ears, he'd just lost it.

Attacking had been his response. A primitive, instinctive response to protect what was his.

Only Piper didn't think she was his.

They'd kissed. So what? If he was going to build anything with her, he had a hell of a lot more work to—

The stair squeaked. The fourth stair from the bottom. It always squeaked when someone was on it. It had squeaked last night and alerted him to Piper slipping down the stairs. Was she going for another midnight snack? He turned and hurried toward the stairs.

Holy hell.

Eric staggered to a stop when he saw her. Piper was wearing his shirt again. She'd picked up plenty of new clothing that day, but she was wearing his white button-down and looking like every fantasy he'd ever had.

When she saw him, Piper froze. Her hand was on the banister. Her feet on the last stair.

He tried a smile. One that he hoped didn't look crazy as all hell. "Got another craving?"

She gave a slow nod. Her hair slid over her cheek.

He closed in on her. "What's it going to be tonight? More chocolate chip cookie dough? Or maybe chocolate? You want to try something different?"

Again, she nodded. "Something different." Her voice was soft. Sexy and husky, and it stroked right over his skin. His cock was already at full attention, mostly because her legs were on glorious, perfect display for him.

And he remembered far too well what it had been like to have her legs wrapped around his hips. For him to carry her across the kitchen. Put her on the table.

I wanted to make a feast of her.

His cock shoved at the front of his pants. Desire beat in his blood, and when he spoke, his voice was gravel rough. "Tell me what you want, and I'll get it for you." Anything to take the fear from her eyes. Eric turned away, ready to hit the kitchen—

"You."

The whole freaking world stopped in that instant. Even his heart stopped beating. Silence lingered all around him.

"Eric? Did you hear me?"

Hell, yes, he had.

But he wanted to make sure he wasn't dreaming. He'd had a dream like this before. A time or twenty.

Her soft footsteps padded toward him. Then her gentle fingertips pressed to his shoulder. "You're what I crave."

If he turned around, he'd devour her. He'd take her and never let go. She didn't realize what she was doing.

What she was offering to a starving man.

He tried to concentrate on breathing. In and out. But he just pulled in her scent and wanted her even more.

"Don't you want me?" Her hand fell away. "You said you did. You kissed me like you did. You made me think—"

He spun toward her. "I want you. Never doubt that."

Her gaze searched his.

"But I'm not some gentle, easy lover." She'd had two lovers. *Two.* Sure, he wanted to kick their asses, and he didn't like thinking about them. But

Piper was careful. She'd chosen those two men. Now she was choosing him.

"I never thought you would be. I thought you'd be rough. Wild. And hot."

His eager cocked jerked toward her. "Why?"

"Because that's pretty much how you always are—"

She was going to make him insane. "*Baby*, why do you want me in your bed, now? What's changed?"

Her lower lip trembled. "I'm scared."

"Being scared isn't a good reason to fuck me."

She flinched.

Shit, shit, shit. He'd done it again. Why did he *always* say the wrong thing to her?

But Piper lifted her chin. "It is if being with you makes me feel safe. If touching you makes me forget the fear and just feel pleasure. That's what happens, Eric. I touch you, and my body ignites. Why can't that be good enough? Why can't I be—"

His hands closed around her shoulders, and he hauled her close. "You are too good for me." Always had been. He'd known that for so long. But...

Now that he was touching her...

Now that she was pressed to his body...

Now that she was staring up at him with need in her golden eyes.

He was a goner.

He kissed her. Took her mouth with a firestorm of need and shoved his good intentions out of the door. She was what he wanted. What he'd always craved. There would be no going back. Not for either of them.

He pulled her up against him, lifting Piper easily and holding her close. He feasted on her mouth. Kissed her deep and hard and loved the soft moan that rolled in the back of her throat. That moan was good, but by the time he was done with her, Eric intended to have her screaming his name as she came for him over and over again.

His tongue thrust into her mouth. Her nipples shoved through the front of the shirt — his shirt — and he wanted those nipples in his mouth. He wanted her. Every single, delectable inch of her.

Eric carried Piper back into his study. The fire was still blazing, dancing and flickering, and he ignored it as he took her to his desk. He put her on the edge of the desk, then caged her with his hands. He kept kissing her. She was kissing him back just as wildly. Her hands curled around his shoulders as she held on tight.

"I want to fuck you," Eric rasped.

"Good…because that's exactly what I want to do with you."

He kissed her again. Fucking hell, he couldn't get enough of her.

His hands rose from the desk. Moved to her silken thighs. He parted her legs, stepped between them, and he shoved up the edges of the shirt so that he could see —

Fuck, fuck, fuck.

"Eric?"

He'd fisted the material of the shirt. "You aren't wearing panties." Not even the sexy ones that she'd bought at the lingerie store.

"I'm kind of an all or nothing woman."

She was wearing *nothing* beneath the shirt. No panties and no bra. That was why her sexy nipples were pushing toward him so clearly.

"I wanted to be all in so, um, I thought if you said yes, then having no panties would make things easier—" Her words ended in a gasp. Then a moan. Because, yes, things were easier.

So much easier.

He could touch what he wanted. Stroke what he craved. Thrust his fingers into her. Strum her clit. Work her hard with his fingers as he'd fantasized about doing over and over again.

Her head tipped back. Her breath came faster. Her hips pushed against him as she rocked into his touch.

She was so responsive. So sensitive. She was going to come. He was going to make her come right then and there, and he'd never been more turned on in his entire life.

He pushed her back on the desk, slid her back more and widened her legs. He dropped his mouth and put it on her sex — a shaved, *silky soft* heaven. He licked her and kissed her and made a meal of her as she—

Screamed.

Screamed his name and came. Hell, yes.

Hell. *Yes.*

But he didn't stop. He couldn't stop. He'd needed her too long. He kept licking and stroking her with his fingers and his tongue as she arched toward him.

"Eric! I'm going—again—"

He wanted her to come again. Again and again. Until pleasure was all she knew. Until he was all she knew. The other two lovers she'd had in the past would be forgotten. Those bastards had been lucky to touch her, a gift they'd never get again. He'd erase them from her memory. He wasn't her first lover, but he'd been her first kiss. And he'd soon know exactly how she liked to be touched and stroked, and he'd never forget. Not a single, solitary thing.

Not when it came to Piper.

His Piper.

Her body stiffened. Her nails bit into his shoulders. "Eric, I want you *in* me!"

She was about to come again. His dick was rock hard. She wanted him in?

He ripped open his pants. His eager cock surged toward her. He thrust into her, sinking balls deep, flesh to flesh.

And it was perfect. Paradise. She was hot and wet and tight. He pulled back, only to thrust in again. Hard. Deep. Over and over. He pounded into her as she came, screaming his name again, raking her nails down his back, biting through the shirt he wore. There was no stopping. No holding back. He'd held back too long. Too many years. Maybe his whole life. He'd always wanted her. Always thought she was out of reach.

She wasn't out of reach any longer. He was balls deep in her. She was screaming his name.

She. Was. His.

And he was hers. Completely. Totally.

But then, he fucking had been…since he'd been seventeen and he'd kissed her in the rain.

Eric's climax exploded, surging through his whole body on an eruption of pleasure that beat in his veins. His very soul. The pleasure consumed him, blinded him, gutted him, and it was the best orgasm of his entire life.

On and on, the pleasure lingered. Blazed. And he held her as tightly as he could.

Piper. His Piper.

He'd just fucked Piper.

The drumming of his heartbeat finally slowed. His breath heaved in and out of his lungs, and he realized that he was holding her hips, gripping them tightly. Probably too tightly. He didn't want to bruise her. He'd *known* he should be careful and handle her with care. Always care. But his hunger had erupted and now—

"I'm sorry."

The words tore from him as Eric lifted up and stared down at Piper. Her eyes were closed, but at his rumbled words, her long lashes lifted.

"For what?"

I fucked Piper.

On his desk.

And he was still mostly dressed. She still had on his shirt. Shit. This whole scene should have gone down way differently. He started to pull out of her, because, yes, greedy bastard that he was, he was still inside of Piper.

Inside of Piper. Flesh to flesh.

No condom.

"I didn't use anything." He backed away. Shoved his still eager cock back in his pants. "Piper—"

"I'm on birth control. And I'm clean."

"So am I. You don't fucking have to worry about that." He'd attacked her like a starving man. Because when it came to her, he *was* starved. Famished. He'd wanted her for years and fought that need. Then she'd come to him. She'd chosen him.

I hope I didn't screw this up. "Did I hurt you?"

She lifted her body so that she was sitting on the edge of the desk once more. She'd been sprawled across it while he took her, and he'd never forget that gorgeous sight.

But she hadn't answered him. "Piper, did I hurt you?"

"No." Her gaze darted over him. "I'd like to go again."

She'd like to —

He grabbed the side of the desk and held on with all of his strength. It was either that, or —

"Do you want to go again, Eric? I mean, I know guys can't always—"

"I can, not a problem." Not even a mild problem. When you'd wanted a woman for as long as he'd wanted her, getting your dick up wasn't a challenge. His dick was up. Up and hard and ready to go again and again.

But this time, he was going to use more finesse. This time, he'd show her care.

This time, he'd at least get her shirt off. *Goal.* He wanted to lick her nipples. Wanted to caress every single inch of her.

And he wanted to make love to her in a bed. Make love, not just fuck her. Because she was someone who mattered.

The one who mattered most.

He scooped her into his arms, and Piper gave a little gasp. "What are you doing?"

"Carrying you." Holding her. Keeping her close.

"Um, yeah, I can walk."

They were already at the stairs. "But I really like having you in my arms." She fit. She was warm and soft, and she eased a tension inside of him that he hadn't even realized was there. He'd been restless, searching for something for so long.

When all that time, what he'd needed most was close by.

The fourth stair groaned beneath his feet.

"If you drop me while you are pulling this Rhett Butler routine, I will never forgive you."

"I'd never drop you." His hold tightened.

She leaned up and pressed a kiss to his neck. Then she licked him. "Do I get to taste this time?"

Okay, he almost stumbled. "Hell, yes." And he double-timed it up those stairs as Piper's warm, sexy laughter filled his ears.

In moments, they were upstairs. In his room because he'd long dreamed of having her sprawled in his bed. He put her down on top of the black, silk sheets, and she smiled at him. As he watched, her hand went to the front of her shirt—it was definitely hers now, he wanted her to keep it forever—and she slowly undid the buttons. The shirt fell away, revealing her breasts.

He stood near the side of the bed, telling himself over and over again...*Don't pounce. Don't act desperate.* He could have tact. He could have control. He could have restraint.

She dropped the shirt over the side of the bed.

Piper was completely naked. Totally and completely.

He was in such trouble because she was absolutely perfect. Rounded breasts, dusky, tight nipples. Flaring hips.

And she was moving toward him. She put her hands on his shoulders as she rose to her knees and stared at him. "You have on way too many clothes."

He swallowed. Twice. "I can fix that problem."

Her smile was pure, wicked temptation. "So can I." Her hands moved to his shirt front. He thought she'd undo the buttons but Piper grabbed the material and yanked—

Buttons flew.

"Whoops." She winked at him.

And even with desire nearly swallowing him whole, Eric felt a laugh escape his lips. "God, Piper—"

She put her mouth on his nipple. Licked. Sucked. Her hands slid down to his waist. She jerked open his pants, and his cock sprang toward her. Her fingers closed around him, stroking and pumping from base to tip, and Eric had to squeeze his eyes shut because he was pretty sure he was about to go out of his freaking mind.

She worked her way down, kissing a path along his chest, over his abs, his stomach, then angling lower so that her mouth closed around the tip of his cock—

Holy. Fuck.

So much for staying in control. He actually felt his control rip away. A snarl broke from him as his fingers closed around her shoulders. If her mouth stayed on him much longer, he'd come. He didn't want to come this way. Well, hell, yes, he did, but he wanted to make sure she reached her orgasm, too, and he hadn't even started to get her close to her climax.

Her tongue swiped over the head of his erection.

He lost it.

Eric closed his hands around her shoulders and pushed her back onto the bed.

"But I wasn't finished!"

He couldn't manage a coherent response to her. He might have growled. Probably snarled some more. Whatever.

He pinned her arms over her head. Held them there with one hand. His cock was already lodged between her thighs, ready to drive inside, but he didn't go in, not yet. With his other hand, he stroked her clit, rubbing her over and over the way he'd already learned she liked. Just the right pressure, just the right speed, just the right—

She arched up against him, and his cock sank deep.

So much for slow. So much for careful. He was driving in and out of her as fast as he could go. Sinking deep. Plunging hard. Her legs wrapped around his hips as he took her mouth in a ferocious kiss. The silken sheets slipped beneath him as he drove into her, over and over, and she came, her sex contracting around him with the ripples of her orgasm.

He poured into her, firing on another orgasm so intense his whole body quaked.

And he kissed her. Kissed her with a hunger that he was fearing would never be sated. Just as the wild desire he felt for her — he wasn't sure that desire would ever end.

Once, he'd told himself that if he ever had Piper, if he ever got her beneath him or on top of him — or any way he could freaking get her — the fascination she held for him would end.

The challenge would vanish.

She'd just go back to being…Piper.

Not the woman who haunted him. Not the woman who invaded his dreams.

He'd been so wrong.

She was always going to haunt him. She *was* his dream.

He withdrew from her. Rose. Stared down at her. Then, without a word, he turned and headed for the bathroom. He had a claw-footed tub in there, a big, giant beast of a tub. One that could easily hold two people. He turned on the water, let the steam drift into the air, and then he exhaled slowly.

Stay in control this time. The third time was the charm, wasn't that the old saying?

He headed back into his bedroom. Only…

His bed was empty.

What the fuck?

And the bedroom door was open.

"*Piper!*" He hadn't meant to bellow her name. Okay, maybe he had. And maybe he had meant to run after her, but when she whirled in the hallway, staring at him with wide eyes and the faintest trace of fear in her golden stare, he got his shit back in check. Fast.

"Baby…" Okay, his voice was lower and way more controlled. He was *never* the type to bellow. Or at least, he hadn't been. He'd just panicked for a moment. "Why did you leave?"

She'd put back on the white shirt. Only buttoned one button. "Uh…I thought we were done. You left."

Done? Ha. "I was just getting a bath ready. I figured you'd like a soak."

She tugged on her left ear lobe. "You aren't…done?"

Not even close. "Are you?"

Her eyes held his.

He stopped breathing.

Her hand dropped as she shook her head. "No. I'm not."

He lifted her into his arms again.

Piper laughed. "You have to stop carrying me!"

But she was small and sexy, and he liked having her in his arms.

Her arms twined around his neck, and her legs curled around his hips. Truly, the perfect position. He kissed her as he turned and took her back into his bedroom. He kept kissing her, and he carried Piper into the bathroom.

He kicked the door shut behind them as steam filled the air.

***

The bastard had money. He lived in a freaking mansion, and the place was surrounded by security. The cameras were easy enough to spot, and, as he scanned the house through his binoculars, he knew that it would be a mistake to get too close.

Piper was inside. Inside with Eric Wilde.

Lights were on—downstairs and upstairs.

They were still awake.

What were they doing?

Fucking?

Piper shouldn't let anyone else touch her. Piper had been meant for him. If she'd given in and screwed that other bastard…Piper would pay.

He'd chosen her. He'd waited for her. He'd intended to put the world at her feet.

She should have turned to him. Should have needed *him*.

She would only get one more chance. He'd let her have one more chance…to leave that big house, to come from behind the walls, to come to *him*.

And if she didn't…

Then he'd destroy the bastard who'd tried to take her from him.

CHAPTER NINE

Something was on top of her. Something warm and heavy stretched across her stomach, and Piper frowned even before her eyes opened. Her hand rose, and she shoved at the offending object—

She touched something warm. A little hairy.

An...arm?

Her eyes flew open. An arm was across her stomach. A tanned, muscled arm. An arm that—as her wide eyes followed it—led back to...Eric. A sleeping Eric. Because she was still in his bed. They were both still naked. Only it wasn't night any longer.

Bright sunlight fell onto the bed. Onto her. And Piper realized exactly what she'd done.

She'd slept with her best friend's brother.

The enemy. The bane of her teenage existence.

The...best lover she'd ever had.

Her eyes squeezed closed. Last night, the plan had seemed like a good one. She knew Eric didn't want any kind of future with her. Eric wasn't the future type. How many times had Ben told her the guy was a playboy who wouldn't settle down with anyone?

Since settling down wasn't on her agenda, either, she'd been totally fine with that. And she'd been afraid. Piper had never particularly enjoyed that emotion. Who did? She'd been afraid, and sexy Eric had been downstairs. She'd already known that they had insane chemistry. When they touched, her whole body did a wild, freak-out thing.

So why not give in to the desire they both felt? What could it possibly hurt?

She'd expected to have sex with him once. A one and done kind of thing.

They'd had sex…three times. Maybe four? Things had gotten a little hazy at the end. And now she was still in his bed. His arm was over her, as if the guy was chaining her to his side, and in the bright light of day, her killer plan suddenly seemed very, very flawed.

What in the hell am I supposed to do next?

She needed to make a hasty exit, one that occurred *before* Eric opened his eyes. They had crossed so many lines the night before. Like, every single line out there. When Ben found out that she'd slept with his brother, the guy was going to flip out. Ben would think Eric had seduced her. Ben frequently called his brother a player.

Only Eric hadn't been the one to seduce her. She'd gone to him. She'd been the one to take the big step. To put the offer out there. Jeez, she'd gone down the stairs without her underwear!

Barely breathing, she carefully caught the edge of Eric's fingers and lifted them up, moving his arm off her a few precious inches. Good. *Good*. This was working. As soon as his arm was off her, she slid out of the bed like a snake and jumped to her feet. As fast as she could, she lowered his hand so that it was cradling the pillow. Her eyes stayed on his face. *His* eyes remained closed. His breathing seemed nice and easy. Still sleeping. Excellent.

She saw the shirt she'd worn the night before, and Piper scooped it up as she made a beeline for the door. She shouldered the shirt on, pushed her arms through the sleeves, haphazardly fixed two of the buttons, and then reached for the bedroom doorknob.

"That was fun." His low, rumbling voice froze Piper in her tracks.

Fun. She felt her cheeks burn.

"Do you always try sneaking out of a lover's bed in the morning? Or is the tip-toe routine something special for me?"

Uh, oh. He sounded pissed. She whipped around and saw that he was already sitting up in bed, arms crossed over his chest and eyes narrowed. Definitely pissed.

"Just for you?" Her words came out as a question, but, yes, she had only done this routine with him.

His jaw clenched.

She'd given him the wrong answer.

"Why?"

She tugged on her ear lobe. "I, um, didn't want to wake you."

His gaze seemed to soften a little. "I got that. But your cheeks are flushed crimson and you were practically *running* away." A pause. "Why are you regretting what happened so soon?"

She twisted her hands in front of her. "It's...you."

He climbed from the bed. Naked. Her eyes closed. Opened for a peek. Closed again. He was aroused. Already. That was a man thing, though. They always woke up ready to go. Didn't they?

The floor creaked. He was stalking toward her. "Put on pants," she squeaked without opening her eyes.

"You didn't want the pants on last night. I sure as hell didn't want them on, either." But she heard the rustle of clothing. He was putting them on. "Why the change of heart?"

She cracked open one eye. Then another. He'd found a pair of jeans that he'd hauled onto his body, and the jeans hung low on his hips. His hair was tousled, his jaw still clenched, and his chest deliciously bare. Jumping him again was certainly an option. Not the best option, but a tempting one.

He took a slow, gliding step toward her. "Piper? Why are you trying to do the walk of shame escape with me? Because, sweetheart, we didn't do anything wrong. There is *nothing* to be ashamed about."

"Right. We're two consenting adults. We had an attraction. We acted on it." She hoped her voice sounded normal. All cool and casual. "I just need to go get dressed now. There's a lot to do." A nightmare she didn't want to think about. She'd escaped the nightmare last night by jumping him.

But now, Piper realized she'd only made a bigger mess. Because it hadn't been some one and done deal for her. In fact, she wanted him now even more than she had before.

Before, she'd only imagined what sex with Eric would be like. Hot. Rough. Wild.

After last night, though, now she knew *exactly* what sex with Eric was like. And, yes, it was hot, it was rough, and it was definitely wild. It was also amazing. Toe-curling. Mind-numbing. Ecstasy that hit in wonderful, never-ending waves.

It was the best kind of sex—and the most dangerous kind. Because it was the addictive kind. The kind where you started to think that maybe, just maybe, you'd found the right lover.

The only lover?

"Is this about Ben?" He took another step toward her. Only this time, the step seemed a wee bit menacing.

Ben. She winced at the name. When Ben found out, *if* Ben found out, he was going to think she'd gone absolutely crazy. "Do we have to tell him?"

Wrong thing to say. Absolutely, completely wrong. She knew that based on the way Eric's whole expression turned straight to stone.

He closed the last bit of distance between them and towered over her. All big, rough, and sexy. "You want me to be your dirty little secret?"

She shook her head. "There isn't really anything little about you. And you're not particularly dirty. Though a few of things you said last night were…fun, in a naughty way."

His dark eyes narrowed even more. "You're not going to make me laugh so that I'll stop being pissed at you. You might be the only fucking person who *can* make me laugh most days, but it's not working today."

She could make him laugh? Well, yes, now that she thought about it, he did have a tendency to laugh more when he was with her. When he wasn't snapping, anyway.

"Ben will fucking know. The whole world will fucking know." He leaned in closer. "Because I don't want anything about our relationship secret."

"We…have a relationship? I thought it was just one night of sex?"

He wasn't laughing, and she hadn't meant her questions to be any kind of joke. Piper was truly confused. What did he want from her?

A muscle flexed along his clenched jaw.

"You don't have relationships," she whispered. "You have lovers that you never stay with. Women who come in and out of your life. You focus on work. You don't look for anything lasting."

"How the hell do you know that?"

She licked her lips. His gaze dropped straight to her mouth and lingered. "Ben."

A hot fury lit his dark stare. "He told you things about me?"

"He just…mentioned you weren't the kind of guy to ever get serious. That you weren't looking for a commitment." She straightened her shoulders. "And I'm not either. That's the last thing I want, so you don't need to worry that I'm going to pull some stage seven cling routine this morning. I don't want commitment. Commitments don't last." She'd learned that bitter truth when she'd been a teenager. "I like to live in the moment." That was where she flourished. If she looked to the past, it hurt too much. And if she looked to the future, it was way too uncertain. Her mother had thought her whole life was mapped out. The husband. The family. The happily ever after.

Then everything had burned to ash around her.

"Don't plan on forever." Those had been her mother's words on the very night she died. Slurred words. Piper had tried to get her mother's keys. She'd tried to stop her mother from going to yet another bar. But...

Stop it, Piper. Don't look to the past.

She squeezed her eyes shut.

And felt a hand brush over her cheek. "Baby, you're crying."

No, no, she could *not* be crying in front of Eric. It was bad enough that she was stumbling her way through the morning after routine, but to break down and cry in front of him? Horror.

She sucked in a deep breath and forced her gaze to lift. "You don't have to worry that I'm looking for a promise or commitment from you. We're attracted to each other. We both had needs last night. What happened between us was wonderful—it was fabulous and sexy, and I have zero regrets." There. Now she was back on track.

He brushed away her tear. "I have zero regrets, too."

Good to know. Her chin notched up.

"Well, I do have one." His hand slid down to cup her chin.

"Wh-what's that?"

"That you tried to slip away. You don't need to do that. I like having you in my bed. I like being close to you." He leaned forward. His lips brushed over hers. "And I'd like more."

Piper swallowed. "More?"

"You really think one night is all that I want from you?"

Her gaze searched his. And, being one hundred percent honest, she told him, "I have no idea what you want from me."

Another soft kiss. "You will."

Before he could say anything else, a quick beeping sound seemed to echo around them. He stiffened, then swore, and alarm flared through Piper. "What's happening?"

"Someone is here."

He grabbed for his phone. His fingers flew across the screen. She knew all of his security feeds could come through on his phone and—

"Ben. He's heading for the gate."

When she peered at Eric's phone, she could see Ben's car pulling up the drive. Oh, crap.

As she watched, Ben braked. Got out. Typed in a code at the gate. Because, of course, he had the code to Eric's place. They were brothers, after all.

I had sex with my best friend's brother.

She looked up from the phone. Eric was staring straight at her.

"You'll want to get dressed," he said, voice emotionless.

No, she wanted to run downstairs and meet Ben while she was just wearing a shirt. Hell, yes, she wanted to get dressed.

"I'll let him in," Eric told her, eyes seeming a little…hard.

"Why is he here so early?"

"Because I had more questions for him. I told him to come by. But that was a plan we made last night." A grim shake of Eric's head. "I didn't realize you and I would be busy with other things."

Other things. Awesome sex. Morning after awkwardness. Check, double check. She whirled for the door.

"You don't have to be embarrassed about what happened."

Her shoulders stiffened.

"I'm sure as hell not embarrassed," he added.

No, he didn't sound embarrassed.

"I wanted you for a long time, Piper. Now that I've had you…"

She risked a glance over her shoulder.

He smiled at her. The slow, toe-curling smile that flashed the hard slash in his cheek. "Now I know exactly what I've been missing all these years."

And she knew exactly what she'd been missing out on, too.

"Piper." A warning edge entered his voice as his smile faded. "I won't be making the same mistake again."

"Mistake?"

"No more hands-off. No more staying back. You want me? You got me."

***

Eric opened the door for his brother, and Ben barreled inside, all tension and fury and questions.

"How is Piper? God, did she sleep at all last night? Her gallery. Her fucking gallery. Do the cops know when the creep broke into the building? Did your team learn anything? Tell me that we've got some camera footage of this asshole—"

Eric held up his hand. He'd dragged on a t-shirt to go with his jeans before he'd hauled ass downstairs. He hadn't bothered with shoes or socks, and he knew stubble coated his jaw. "Slow down, man. I haven't even had coffee yet."

Ben's blue eyes blazed. "Screw coffee. I need to know about Piper. How is she?"

Eric shut the front door. Locked it. How was Piper? *Better than every single dream I had.* "She's showering. Getting dressed. She'll be down here soon." He should get some coffee for her. The woman loved her morning brew. He turned and headed for the kitchen, with Ben following behind him.

"I should have come over last night. I feel like a total ass for not being with her."

"I told you not to come." Because he'd thought Piper was exhausted. That she just wanted to crash.

She'd wanted other things. So had he.

"This is so bad." Ben sat at the bar. "I know how much the gallery means to her. This bastard—torching her home, destroying her art. It's personal. So freaking personal, and it scares the hell out of me." He glanced over his shoulder, as if to make sure Piper wasn't there. "You need to know more about Grady. I know I told you a bit about him yesterday, but there's more."

Grady. His team was already checking on the guy.

"He's…come sniffing around some since they broke up. He, fuck, he came after me a few times."

Eric's hands flattened on the bar. "What?"

Ben winced. "That's the thing, see…the guys that she blows off, they think it's because—because she's involved with someone else. And the guy who is always in her life?"

"You." Hell.

Ben's nod was slow. "When she won't commit to them, and they see her out on the town with me…they think I'm the problem. They think I'm the one standing in their way." He exhaled. "Grady came after me twice. The first time, it was a year after they'd broken up. Asshole found me at a bar and started talking all kind of trash. Saying that he'd known Piper was screwing around on him the whole time." Ben shook his head. "Piper thought he was easy going. Fun. And he was…until he *wasn't*. Know what I mean?"

"You said the *first* time. Tell me about what happened the *other* time." Tension coiled heavily in his gut.

"Piper was staying at my place. She does that, you know?"

Yeah, he knew.

"Grady must have been watching her. He came to the house, banging in the middle of the night. I opened the door, and he took a swing at me."

Every muscle in Eric's body locked down. "And you didn't think to mention this shit sooner? Like when you were fucking briefing me on the guy yesterday?"

"He's all the way across the country! He lives in LA now! When he came that night, I knocked his ass out. Told him to stay the hell away from Piper. To never contact her or me again." He scraped a hand over his jaw. "And he hasn't. At least, I don't think he has."

Eric took out his phone. Sent a text to Simon. *I want to know where the hell Grady Fox is right now. He just moved to the top of our suspect list.*

"Piper looks for the best in people, you know? And that's a good thing. Usually. Because I swear, she can make people be better." Ben huffed out a breath. "Jesus, she even looks for the best in you. Can you believe that shit? Even though she knows you're a dick most days, she's always telling me that I'm lucky to have you."

Eric's hold on the phone tightened. "Piper doesn't have any family."

"Well, her prick of a father is out there, somewhere."

He knew exactly where her father was. A story for another day.

"He hasn't reached out to her since he left her mom. You know that jerk didn't even show up for the funeral. She doesn't have any siblings or cousins..." Ben rolled back his shoulders. "But she has me. I'm her family. The only family she'll ever need."

"No. You're not."

Eric's phone beeped. He'd gotten a text from Simon.

Already on him. According to what I'm learning, the guy should be in LA. Verifying that right now.

Eric heard a faint rustle of sound near the doorway. The light tap of a shoe, and Eric's gaze whipped in that direction.

Piper stood there, her face a bit pale and her blonde hair still a little wet from what had to be a shower of absolute record speed for her. She wore jeans that hugged her like a second skin and a loose, green sweater that skimmed to her thighs. She stared straight at him, and Eric could have sworn there was pain in her eyes. Her lips parted —

"Ben *is* my family." Her voice was flat. "Just because he's not blood, that doesn't mean I don't love him like family."

"Damn straight." Ben jumped from the bar stool and headed for her. He pulled Piper in his arms, squeezing her tight in a bear hug. "I'll always be here for you."

She loved Ben like family.

How does she love me?

Fuck, who was he kidding? Piper didn't love him at all, but she'd still given him her body the night before. She'd come beneath him. On top of him. Her orgasms had made her scream his name.

And he'd have her screaming again when they were alone.

Ben eased back and peered down at Piper. "How'd you sleep? Were you able to get any rest?"

Her gaze jumped to Eric. He just lifted a brow.

"Or did you toss and turn all night?"

Her cheeks flushed. "It was a long night."

"Sure as hell was," Eric murmured.

Frowning, Ben shot him a questioning glare.

Eric turned away, shrugging, as he got the coffee ready. Behind him, he heard Piper's soft steps approach, then the faint screech as she pulled out one of the bar stools. He thought about the last time he'd had her at the bar.

And he got a sudden craving for ice cream.

"I told him about Grady," Ben announced in a rush. "I know you liked to think the guy was all sunshine and roses, but he had a temper, Piper.

And a streak of jealousy in him that ran a mile wide."

Eric knew he had that same damn jealousy. He had to get that shit under control. He eased out a low breath then turned to face Piper. She was at the bar, as he'd figured, and Ben was right behind her. "When was the last time you heard from Grady?"

She bit her lower lip. "It was right after…um, after Ben decked him. What was that? A few years ago?" She shot a quick glance at Ben.

He nodded.

"Grady texted me. Told me that he was sorry for being an ass. Said he wouldn't be bothering me again." A shrug. "And that was it. I haven't heard from him since then."

"He's at the top of the suspect list. You should have told me that he'd gotten violent with you."

"He didn't—"

Eric cut in, saying, "He attacked Ben. Fucking counts as violent."

Her gaze held his. "That was years ago. Why would he wait so long and suddenly start terrorizing me? That doesn't make any sense."

"Every man you dated. Every lover. I need to know *all* the secrets, Piper." A dark anger boiled inside of him. "You can't hold anything back from me. This isn't some game." He leaned toward her. "Your life is on the line."

Her breathing came faster. "I never thought it was a game."

"No? Then don't hold back on me. Don't forget to tell me that your ex, the *easy going one*, took a swing at my brother." Eric shook his head and thought about the damage to her canvases. The fire at her home. "What else are you holding back?" His voice dropped.

"Easy," Ben cautioned.

Eric shook his head. "Hell, no. You've *both* been holding back on me. That shit can't happen. I get that the two of you have always kept your secrets from the rest of the world. But that time is over. No more secrets. No more holding back." His stare focused totally on Piper. "I can't keep you safe if I'm in the dark. What else haven't you told me? What else are you hiding?"

"There's nothing."

"Another lover? Another guy who wanted to get closer but you shut him down?"

Ben put a protective hand on her shoulder. "Okay, man, ease up. Let's all take a breath."

Piper jumped to her feet. "You're acting like I did this. Like I *made* this happen."

"No!" Shit. He yanked a hand through his hair. She was turning and rushing away. He bounded after her. Closed his hand around her shoulder and swung her back to face him. "Someone wants you. Don't you see that? Someone is obsessed. Trying to hurt you. I *can't* let you be hurt."

Behind him, Ben had fallen silent.

Eric released a slow breath, but he didn't let her go. "I have to know what I'm dealing with. If there are more secrets, if these *perfect* assholes from your past did something I need to know about, tell me that shit. I need the truth, not a convenient lie."

"No one is perfect," Piper threw back.

He sure as hell wasn't.

His phone vibrated. With his free hand, he yanked out his phone and saw the text from Simon.

Grady Fox isn't in LA. Just got confirmation. The guy took a private flight to Atlanta last week. He's supposed to be at some kind of tradeshow. But I just talked to the manager at his hotel...Grady paid for a full week, but he hasn't shown up for the last four days.

Fuck.

"Eric? What is it?" Piper demanded.

He glanced up at her. "Grady is back in town."

CHAPTER TEN

"I don't like the way you're looking at Piper, bro."

Eric gaped at the guy. "The way I'm *looking* at her? She's not even freaking here right now!"

They were at Wilde Securities. Piper was down the hallway, looking at footage from one of the traffic cams near her gallery. He'd wanted her to take a look at the cars in the footage, even though all of the plates were being run by his team. Just in case something jumped out at her.

Ben was currently in his office and getting on Eric's last nerve.

Grady was definitely in Atlanta. Simon had tracked the guy's credit card transactions. A team was narrowing down his location.

Eric planned to be having a not-so-friendly chat with the fellow within the hour.

"You know what I'm talking about." Ben's eyes raked him. "Back at your house, you were all up in her space."

Eric just gave a mocking laugh. "My house, my space."

"You *know* what I mean! You were glaring at her. You were pushing her! You grabbed her shoulder and you—"

Now Eric was on his feet. "I didn't hurt her. I would *never* hurt Piper."

"That's fucking bullshit, and we both know it. You broke her heart when she was fifteen, and you treated her like crap after that day."

Shock rolled through Eric. "What?"

Ben marched around the desk and stood toe-to-toe with him. "You think I didn't know? Seriously? Piper couldn't keep a secret to save her life back then! Oh, sure, she tried. But she went from being lit up like a Christmas tree one day…to pretty much sobbing the next. I knew some jerk had broken her heart. I also knew that she used to have one hell of a crush on you. You started avoiding her like the plague—"

I wasn't avoiding her. I was avoiding both of you — mostly because you, dear dumbass of a brother, bragged that she was your freaking first!

"I don't know exactly what went down back then. And I don't want to know. Whatever it was, I knew it was the end for you and Piper."

Hardly. A beginning. A very slow beginning.

"You kept your distance from her for years, and that was great because a guy like you would just burn through her."

He lifted his brows. "A guy like me? What the hell does that even mean?"

"You don't get serious!" Ben practically exploded. Red stained his cheeks. "You don't have room for anything in your life but work. Piper doesn't want that."

"And you know exactly what she wants." Eric thought about the way Piper had gone absolutely wild for him the night before. "Sorry, but this time, you're the one who is clueless. She's a grown woman. She can go after anything or anyone that she wants in her life. Her choice. Not yours. Being her best friend doesn't give you the right to control anything about her."

"I'm not controlling her! I'm helping her!" Ben huffed out a breath. "Just keep your hands off her. Keep your dick zipped away and make sure—"

A soft knock sounded at the office door. The knock came just in time because Eric had opened his mouth to tell Ben just where Piper liked for him to keep his dick, and it *wasn't* zipped away.

The door opened and Piper slipped inside. Her gaze darted between the two of them. "Everything all right in here?"

Ben gave a jerky nod. "Just settling some things with my brother."

He hadn't settled jackshit. "Something you need to know, *bro*," Eric began menacingly. "Piper and I—"

Piper's eyes went wide. She winced and seemed to brace herself. She knew he was going to tell his brother what they'd done. And she was...afraid? Hell, yes, she was. Her hand was rising toward her ear.

Screw that. He stalked toward her. Took her hand in his. Squeezed.

Ben cocked his head. "You and Piper—what?"

Eric wasn't going to say a word. She didn't want him spilling? She wanted him to be a dirty secret? Hell, that was fine. If he got to slide into her bed each night—or if she jumped in his—then that would stay between them. He cleared his throat. "We need to go and talk to Simon. He's supposed to have a location on Grady soon, and I want it."

He felt some of the tension slide from Piper. Eric rolled back his shoulders. "Come on, Piper." He led her out of the office, past Dennis and his carefully organized desk, and toward the nearest elevator. As soon as the elevator doors closed behind him—

"Now I'm one of your secrets?" Eric's words were low. "You're not a kid, Piper. You can pick your own lovers, and if my brother doesn't like that we're together, he can screw off."

Of course, Ben wouldn't like it. He'd just made that crystal clear, hadn't he?

"Ben is all I have. My one constant." Her chin dipped toward her chest.

He jabbed a button on the control panel, stopping the elevator right there. "Bullshit."

Her head whipped up.

"He isn't all you have. He *isn't* your family."

Piper sucked in a sharp breath and took a step back.

Oh, no, not happening. He lifted his hands and caged her, placing his palms flat on the elevator wall behind her head. "You think I don't care about you? You think I'm just fucking you for fun?"

Her eyes widened. "It *was* fun."

Hell, yes. "It's more than sex. And he *isn't* all that you have." *I'm right here, Piper. Right in front of you.*

"I know I have plenty of friends." Her lips pressed together. "I'm lucky to have good friends in my life, but Ben is more than that. He has stood by me during my worst moments. He's—" But she broke off, and a furrow appeared between her eyebrows. "You were there."

Eric just waited. As he'd waited for so long.

The faint line between her eyebrows deepened. "When I buried my mom, you were right beside me."

"Where else would I have been?"

"But you hated me back then!"

A grim shake of his head. "Baby, you need to know that I have never hated you. I could never hate you."

Still seeming a bit dazed, Piper said, "When I graduated college, you were there."

He leaned in close. "Someone had to clap."

"Ben brought me roses, but you—"

"*I* brought the fucking roses. Ben just gave them to you because I figured if I handed them to you, you'd throw them in the trash."

Her eyes widened. "I wouldn't have done that."

Good. "Think about the times in your life, Piper. When things are good, I'm there. When things are bad, I am there even faster. Because I will always be there. You've been a fixture in my life for as long as I can remember, but unlike Ben, I don't want to just be your friend."

"What do you want?"

"Everything." His lips lowered and pressed to her lips. A soft kiss. A tender one. He wanted her. Wanted to claim her. Wanted to make her laugh. Wanted to protect her. Wanted to grow old with her at his side.

Was that so much to ask?

He just wanted forever, and he was working hard to get it.

First step…get rid of her stalker.

Second stop…Eric was going to try and get Piper to fall for him.

He let the kiss linger a moment longer because kissing Piper was one of the true pleasures in life. Her hands rose to press to his chest. A delicious moan trembled in the back of her throat.

He would have enjoyed fucking her right then and there. Eric put that item on the to-do list.

Piper in an elevator. Piper anywhere and everywhere. But first…

Get rid of the stalker.

He pulled back. Put some much-needed space between them because his dick was shoving hard against the front of his pants. His hand flew out and slammed into the control panel, starting the elevator again. "When you're safe, I'm going to tell you exactly what I want. And hopefully, you'll give it to me."

She swallowed. "I feel like I don't really know you."

"Maybe you don't." She'd just seen the image he projected. The guy who'd spent years trying to keep his hands off her because he thought she was meant for someone else.

But Piper wasn't sleeping with Ben. And she was staring at *him* with need in her golden eyes.

The elevator dinged. The doors opened.

Piper's lips parted—

"What the hell happened?" Simon demanded.

Eric growled.

"Did the elevator get stuck? I was about to call in maintenance."

Eric turned to face his VP. And he saw the faint laughter gleaming in the guy's eyes. Using his body as a shield, Eric lifted his hand and let one of his fingers do the talking for him.

Simon choked out a laugh.

"Did you find him?" Piper's voice. Strained. She hurried from the elevator, and Eric followed her out.

All signs of laughter left Simon's face. "Yes, we think we found him. Turns out, the guy rented a house just down the street from your home. One of those online rental things. That's how we tracked him—we saw the credit card purchase come up. I've got a team outside the location right now because his rental car is there—another ding on the credit card—and they're making sure he doesn't leave until we get to the scene."

Anticipation had Eric rocking forward. "Let's go."

Simon nodded, looking satisfied. "Knew you'd want to be the first to question him."

Eric headed forward, but Piper's hand flew out and curled around his wrist. "Shouldn't we call the cops?"

"We don't have evidence tying the guy to anything yet," Simon told her as his lips twisted. "But Eric and I tend to be pretty good at getting perps to trip up and confess."

Her eyes searched Eric's. "I want to be there."

"Oh, no," Simon said immediately. "Bad plan. You're the target of this guy's obsession. If he sees you, then he might flip out."

Her chin notched. "*If* he's obsessed, then me being there could be a good thing. Maybe I can throw him off his game. Get him to speed up that whole confession bit."

Eric knew this plan was bad—and there was no way he was putting her at risk. "Or he sees you, and he attacks. Maybe he's got accelerants in that place just like he used on *your* home. He sees you and torches the house he's renting. Or he tries to torch *you*." No way. "We don't let civilians go out on cases like these, baby. It's for your safety."

"Civilians?" Her brows rose. "You're a civilian."

Technically, yeah, he was. Though he'd done plenty of side work for Uncle Sam over the years.

Simon gave a low whistle. "Don't worry, Piper. I assure you that Eric knows how to play plenty rough and dirty." Again, laughter slipped from him. "She has no idea who you really are, does she?"

His words were too close to the conversation in the elevator.

Eric saw that truth sink in for Piper. No, she didn't really know him. Didn't know what he'd been doing all these years. He hadn't just been sitting behind a desk. Hadn't just been inventing tech and counting his millions as they rolled in.

He'd gotten his hands dirty plenty of times. Like Simon, he'd even started to crave the rush of adrenaline that came from the hunt. But there was one thing he craved more than the adrenaline…

And she was glaring at him. "I don't like this."

Eric kissed her. "I'll be back before you know it. If he's guilty, I'll make sure Grady is locked away."

"Eric—"

He saw the approaching agents behind her back. Julia and Rick. "Talk to Julia. Make sure you've seen all the footage we took from your gallery." Because they'd been able to retrieve surveillance footage before the asshole had cut the system. A damn good cut job because the perp had known how to sever the security without sending out an alarm. "I'll be back before you know it."

A hard shake of her head. "I don't like this."

He wasn't going to risk her. Another kiss, and then he headed down the hallway with Simon. He didn't look back, but he was pretty sure he could feel Piper's glare burning right through his skin.

Simon didn't talk to him again, not until they were in the parking garage, and Eric was behind the steering wheel of the Benz.

Then Simon gave a patently false cough. "Um, you kissed her."

Eric shifted the car into reverse. "Yes."

"That mean you two are a thing? This case get personal for you?"

A jerky nod. It hadn't just become personal. It always had been.

Silence from Simon. And then… "Does she have any idea what you'd do for her?"

No, and, hopefully, she wouldn't ever have to find out.

***

Julia's caramel eyes were wide. Rick was frowning at her. Looking at her like Piper had two heads. She didn't—just the one. Piper rolled back her shoulders. "Where is the video footage?"

"This way." Julia pointed down the hallway. To the left.

Rick kept frowning. "You and the boss...together?" His voice was deep and rumbling, and the guy bore a very close resemblance to Vin Diesel. Next to him, Julia was petite and charming, a bundle of energy and...in that moment, shock.

But Julia wasn't asking if Piper was involved with the boss. Though, judging by Julia's expression, the woman didn't need to ask.

Crap. The kiss had been far too public—both kisses. And Eric hadn't seemed to care who saw them.

Luckily, Ben hadn't been there. Ben hadn't seen.

Does it really matter if he does?

The question slipped through her mind, and Piper wondered...just what was she protecting? *Who* was she protecting?

Julia elbowed her partner as she got her surprise under control. "You don't get to ask questions like that. It's not tactful. How many times have I told you that you have got to get more tact?"

Rick shrugged his massive shoulders. His tense expression said he didn't give a shit about tact.

A long sigh escaped Julia. "Come on, Piper. I'll show you the footage."

Piper followed her into one of the rooms down the hallway. She didn't *want* to follow Julia, though. She wanted to run after Eric. To go with him to confront Grady.

But, yes, she got why Eric wanted her to stay behind. Only she wasn't the staying behind type.

Just as they neared the small room, Ben appeared. He hurried toward her as he double-timed it down the hallway. "Eric texted me — told me you were down here and that he was going to confront Grady." His jaw clenched. "Wish he'd waited for me."

"Join the club," Piper muttered.

Once inside the room, Julia keyed up the security feed and the monitors to the left began to show Piper's gallery.

"This is footage from nine days ago — the last day the security system worked. Pay attention to the customers and let me know if anyone sticks out in your mind," Julia instructed her.

Piper pulled out a nearby chair and focused on the monitors. She saw her assistant, Jessica, with her long braid of red hair.

"Has Jessica been brought in for an interview?" Ben asked before Piper could. "I mean, she was in the gallery. If someone screwed with the security there, maybe it was an inside job."

Piper started to shake her head.

"We'll be talking to her," Julia cut in. Rick stood silently by her side. "We always start with those closest to the targets. She's out of town now, supposedly down in Florida—"

"Her vacation," Piper added. "She went down to visit her mom in Tampa."

Julia and Rick shared a quick, fast glance.

Uh, oh. "What's wrong?"

Julia winced. "According to the intel we've already gathered on your assistant, Jessica's mother died last year. Wherever she is, she's not with her mother."

CHAPTER ELEVEN

"He would have been able to watch her house perfectly from here." Eric braked his car and eyed the quiet, colonial-style, brick house. The sunlight shone down on the house and on the blue SUV in the drive.

Grady Fox's rental. A rental that had been due back yesterday.

Eric's hold tightened on the steering wheel. "He was right here, and we didn't know it."

Grady had been close enough to watch the blaze. Close enough to watch Piper.

Had he been watching the first night when Eric had taken her away from that very street?

Eric killed the engine and jumped from the vehicle. He'd been sure to park a bit down the road, just as his agents had done.

Simon hurried to his side. "What's the plan here? Guess we're not going to play things cool, huh?"

Screw cool. Eric stalked toward the house, moving quickly up the broken sidewalk even as his gaze swept the perimeter, looking for any signs of a threat. The windows were closed, and the curtains drawn.

He rolled back his shoulders. His hand skimmed over the hood of the rental. Ice cold. The vehicle hadn't been used recently.

"Not even going to play the good cop, bad cop routine?" Simon's voice was a whisper as he shadowed Eric's movements. "Just going in with guns blazing?"

They were both armed, but no, he didn't intend to fire his way inside.

Why bother, when the door was unlocked?

As soon as he stepped foot on the porch, Eric noticed that the front door was ajar. The lock didn't appear broken in any manner. The door was simply open, a bare inch. As if someone had forgotten to shut it.

"No," Simon muttered. "Not a fucking good sign."

No, it wasn't.

Eric lifted his hand and pounded on the door. "Grady Fox! Grady, my name is Eric Wilde, and I need to talk to you—" The door slid open a bit more beneath his pounding fist.

The smell hit him. It wafted out from the opening in the doorway, and Eric closed his mouth immediately. Dammit, he *knew* that smell.

Behind him, Simon was already cursing.

"We need the cops here," Eric said flatly. "Call Detective Layla Lopez." A cop he knew and trusted. A homicide detective.

After this call, he'd expect the Atlanta PD to be all in on the investigation.

After all, it was pretty hard to ignore a murder. Carefully, he entered the house, making sure not to touch anything. The smell assured him that a body was inside. Decomposition was hard to mistake. But just in case someone else was in the place, he had to take a look.

The body was in the den. Tied to a chair — arms roped down and ankles secured to the legs of the chair. Stab wounds littered the guy's chest and his head sagged forward, dirty blond hair hanging over his forehead.

"That's Grady Fox," Simon muttered. "Poor bastard."

Someone had tortured Grady. Taken slow and careful time with him. Eric knew a torture scene when he saw one, and Simon sure as hell could spot one, too.

Eric also knew a thing or two about lividity. Sure, he was no ME, but judging by the way the body had, um, turned, he suspected Grady had been dead for at least two or three days.

He didn't set the fire at Piper's place. He'd probably been dead long before that happened.

Eric looked at the blood that soaked the guy's body. All of that dark, red blood.

He'd been worried that Piper's stalker would accelerate. The guy already *had* accelerated. He'd committed murder, and there was going to be no going back for the bastard now.

They backed out of the house, and Eric reached for his phone. The stench of the body filled his nose and mouth. He could freaking *taste* that horror. He retreated and dialed the agent he knew he could trust.

Julia answered on the second ring. "Yeah, boss." Her voice was brisk. "What did you find?"

"A dead body. Grady was murdered."

"What?"

"You stick to Piper like glue, understand? You and Rick make sure you're her shadows. Wherever she goes, you follow."

Piper's ex had been brutally murdered—right down the street from her house. A cold knot formed in Eric's stomach.

"Who's the vic?" Julia asked him, her voice completely without emotion.

"The guy who was our number one suspect. Grady Fox."

***

"Who's the vic?"

At Julia's low words, Piper stiffened. She'd been staring at video footage of her gallery, watching the customers come in and out, but as soon as she heard that question from Julia—

Rick swore.

Ben stopped tapping his fingers on the desk.

Piper whirled her chair around so that she could see Julia.

The other woman nodded and kept her easy grip on her phone. "Understood. You can count on us, boss." She ended the call. Her gaze immediately went to Rick. "Protection detail, level six," she said briskly.

He gave an almost imperceptible nod.

"What is happening?" Piper demanded. "Who's the victim?"

She could see Julia trying to decide what to tell her. She wasn't in the mood to be handled, though. Piper just wanted the truth. "Did Eric find Grady?"

Julia swallowed. "Yes."

Now Piper leapt to her feet. "Did Grady hurt someone?" Her heart squeezed in her chest. "Who? Who did Grady hurt? Who—"

"He didn't hurt anyone." Julia's gaze assessed Piper. "I'm sorry, Piper, but Grady is dead. Eric and Simon are calling the cops to the scene now."

Dead? What? Then a new fear hit her. "Eric! He's okay? He's—"

Ben jumped up, too.

But Julia raised a hand. "Eric is fine. He and Simon found the body. I'm sorry, but that's all I know right now."

Piper didn't completely believe her. She thought that was all Julia was willing to share.

"We're your guards," Julia continued doggedly. "Eric wants to make sure we don't let you out of our sight until—"

Piper marched for the door.

"What are you doing?" It was Rick who barked out the question—as he blocked her path. "You need to finish reviewing the footage."

"I reviewed the footage three times already. I told you the names of all the customers there, and I told you the artist who came in to drop off his work is Richard Milo. I told you everything that I knew, and, now, I'm going to find Eric."

Rick shook his head. "He doesn't want you at the scene."

Too bad. "Grady is dead. This whole nightmare is about me. I can't just sit here!"

Ben shuffled closer to her. "Suicide? Is that what happened? The guy was obsessed with Piper and he took his own life?"

Her heart squeezed in her chest.

"It wasn't suicide." Julia's flat answer.

She does know more than she's saying.

Ben gave a rough sigh. "Well, I'm doubting the fellow died of natural causes."

Silence.

A shiver slid over Piper. "I've got level six protection." Whatever the hell that meant—it just sounded intense. "I've got it because Grady was murdered, wasn't he?"

Rick didn't say a word. She'd noticed the guy had a tendency to take the silent routine way too far.

Piper glanced over her shoulder at Julia.

Julia gave a slow nod.

Oh, God. Piper whipped her head back toward Rick. "Get out of my way."

A muscle flexed in his jaw. "I have orders—"

"Come with me then, but I am getting to that scene. Grady is dead? He was murdered?" And—the part that pierced straight to her soul—was the fear that he'd been killed...*because of me.* "Give me the level six protection, fine, but I am getting to that house. I have to know what's happening, and I'm not just going to sit on the sidelines. This is *my* life." A life someone was screwing with.

Murder. How could this be happening? And why? What had she possibly done that had driven someone to kill?

***

Piper wasn't allowed close to the crime scene, but that was hardly a surprise. There was evidence to collect. Procedures to follow. A body to move.

A body...

God!

Grady was dead? Truly? When they arrived at the scene—Piper, Ben, Rick and Julia, a ragtag and tense group—the cops had already been there.

Neighbors were out and gaping at the activity. When she looked down the street, Piper saw her home. The side of her house was still blackened from the fire. Yellow tape blocked off the area.

A white van was at the murder scene. She shivered when she looked at the van. The ME? Piper suspected the body would be transported in that big, shady-looking van. Grady's body.

"What in the hell is she doing here?"

Eric's voice. And just like that, he was in front of her. She'd been gazing at the van, seeing Grady in her mind, and Eric had stalked toward her with his silent steps.

"Level freaking six protection means she isn't exposed to danger! Dammit! Rick, Julia, you both know this shit." Anger rolled in his voice.

Julia stepped toward him. Her gaze held his. "Yeah, well, level six doesn't mean we get to tie the woman to a chair—"

He flinched.

"And keep her captive until you return! She's not under some kind of arrest, and she was demanding to be brought here." Julia's thumb jerked toward Piper. "So we brought her, and we're sticking close, and she's not going to leave without us."

Eric swiped a hand over his face. His gaze slid over Piper. "You shouldn't be here. You don't…you don't want to see him. Not this way. Trust me."

"What happened to Grady?" Her gaze darted to the house's entrance.

A woman strode out, a woman dressed in a black business suit, with her dark hair pulled back in a tight bun. There was a badge clipped to the woman's hip, and when she strode forward, Piper could see the holster under her arm. Simon followed out behind her, and his expression was darker than Piper had ever seen it before.

"He was…stabbed." There as a slight hesitation in Eric's words.

Piper's arms wrapped around her stomach.

Ben's hand brushed over her back in comfort. "How long has he been dead?"

"Maybe three days. That's just my estimate. The ME will tell us for certain."

Three days? He'd been in that house, cold and dead, all that time?

Simon and the mystery woman were heading toward them. The woman's gaze had settled on Piper.

Eric sighed. "Detective Lopez has questions for you, Piper. That's her with Simon. Hell, maybe it is a good thing that you came down here. We can get the questions out of the way, then you can go home."

Her home was currently sectioned off by yellow tape—

"*Our* home," he corrected immediately, a slight edge in his voice.

Ben's hand slid away from Piper.

It wasn't their home. It was his place, and, no, she wasn't just going to run and hide behind the security there. Someone had killed Grady. She needed to do *something*.

The detective had reached their little circle. Her dark stare seemed to assess them all. Her skin was a perfect, warm olive, her lips unpainted and full. Small pearls dotted the lobes of her ears. "Piper Lane?"

She nodded.

"I'm Detective Layla Lopez, and I'm going to need you to come to the station."

"What?" Eric's immediate response. "Why? You can just ask your questions here and—"

"No, I can't." Her calm response. "Because I have a great deal of questions. Because this is a homicide investigation, one that I am managing. And, no, I won't do any favors for you, Eric, despite our past relationship."

Shit. They'd been involved?

The detective lifted one brow in a delicate arch. "This is very serious business."

Of course, it was. It was murder.

The detective's focus was on Piper. "I'll be taking you to the station. Your guards can certainly come along, but you won't be leaving my company, not until all of my questions are answered."

It was Ben who surged forward. "What in the hell? Why are you treating Piper like she did something wrong? She's the target here!'

Detective Lopez shook her head. "She's not the target. *My* victim is the man who was tied to a chair and tortured for what I expect was an extended period of time. He was her ex-lover, and when my techs just opened his computer—a computer that was stashed inside the house—they found an email from Piper."

That wasn't possible. "No," Piper denied. "I haven't contacted him since—"

"The email was dated six days ago. It came from your account at your gallery, and the note specifically asked Grady to come and see you."

Her breath came faster. Desperate, her stare darted to Eric. "I didn't. I swear, I didn't!"

"In the email, you told him that you missed him. That you wanted him back. That you'd even arranged a place for him to stay down here. One close to you." The detective put her hands on her hips. "So, we'll be going down to the station. You'll be answering all of my questions. And, yes, before you even ask, you might want to get yourself a lawyer."

CHAPTER TWELVE

She'd been in a police station before, but Piper had never been a *suspect* at the station. She'd never been interrogated, and it was freaking her the hell out. The interrogation and the *murder.*

"Piper, I'm a divorce attorney. You need someone else." Ben's voice was ragged as he sat beside her. He leaned forward in one of those rickety chairs that you saw on cop shows—only this was real life—because they were waiting to be *interrogated.*

No, not they. She was. She was the suspect. "Do not even think of leaving me."

"I'm not! But I did call in a friend who specializes in criminal law. He'll be here within the hour. Just don't say anything until Kendrick gets here, okay?"

She didn't know where Eric was. Eric, Rick, and Julia had followed her and Detective Lopez to the station, but when she'd been escorted back to the interrogation room, they'd been blocked. Since Ben was a lawyer—she'd declared him to be *her* lawyer in her loudest possible tone — he'd been able to go back with her.

"I didn't do this." She had to swallow twice to clear the dryness from her throat. "Someone is trying to set me up! I would *never* kill Grady!"

"I know." He took her hand and squeezed. "You're not a killer, Piper. I didn't think for one second that you were."

"I didn't send him an email. You know I was out of town! I didn't even have my laptop with me! It's been at my gallery the whole time and —" Her eyes went wide. "Jessica. We have to find her. She had access to my laptop. Maybe she sent the message."

His brow furrowed. "Why?"

"I have no idea!" Her voice had risen because she was losing her shit. And she was scared. Grady was dead, some jerk was terrorizing her, and now she was a murder suspect?

The door opened with a quiet groan. Detective Lopez stood there a moment, her gaze sliding first to Piper, then to Ben, then to their joined hands.

Then she looked over her shoulder, a faint frown on her face as she focused on the man behind her — Eric.

Just seeing him sent a surge of relief through Piper.

"You okay?" Eric asked her, voice quiet.

She shook her head. "Not even close." But she was better than poor Grady. Piper rose to her feet and locked her stare on the detective. "What is happening? I didn't kill Grady—and I didn't send that email!"

"Piper." Ben grabbed her hand and tugged her back down. "I'm your—temporary—attorney, and I'm advising you to remain quiet."

The detective headed into the room with a slow, brisk stroll. She pulled out the chair on the opposite side of the table and took her time getting settled.

Eric stalked inside. He pulled a chair close to Piper and sat next to her. His shoulder brushed against hers.

The detective's brows rose, and she nodded. "Good to know where we all stand."

Ben leaned forward. "Piper isn't a killer. She's—"

"Yes, yes, I'm sure she's all sunshine and light and stardust." The detective rolled her eyes. "Do you know how many men think they know a woman? Like, really think they understand her?" She waved her hand toward Piper. "But they only understand jackshit." She smiled. "The emails were sent from your computer, Ms. Lane. And notice I said *emails*, as in plural."

"Piper," she whispered. It seemed weird to be all formal when the other woman was accusing her of murder.

"I've got all kinds of techs who can figure stuff out for me. They say the notes were definitely sent from *your* computer, from *your* email address."

"You should talk to my assistant," Piper blurted. "Jessica had access to my computer, and she—I just found out that she lied to me. She was supposed to be visiting her mother but—"

Eric's hand closed around her knee and squeezed. She shot him a frown. Why was he stopping her when she was just telling the truth?

The detective cleared her throat, drawing Piper's attention. Then the detective gave her a sweet smile. "How do you know she was visiting her mother?"

"She texted me and said that she was." Piper shook her head. "But she wasn't. Eric's team found out that Jessica's mother died last year."

The detective glanced at Eric. "True," Detective Lopez said. "Her mother did die." A pause. "And so, I'm afraid, did Jessica."

Jessica wasn't dead. Piper shook her head. "No, she's—"

"Her car was found this morning. It had been totaled. Jessica Bromley was inside." A pause. "When did you get the text from her? Exactly?"

Nausea rose within Piper. "She's dead?"

"Yes. I'd like to see your phone, please. I mean, if you have nothing to hide, you can hand it over and let me see this text that you got from her."

"Piper…" Ben's voice held a warning. "Let's wait for Kendrick to get here."

"I don't have anything to hide." She pulled her hand free of Ben's. A moment later, she unlocked her phone's screen and pushed her phone across the table.

The detective scanned through her text messages. Her eyes narrowed. "That's interesting."

"What?"

She looked up at Piper. "You received the text at least a day after she died. According to what we've got from the medical examiner in Florida, anyway. You see, Jessica's body was in that car a while. She'd gone off the road. No one noticed."

Okay, the nausea was worse. So was the fear. And the grief. *Jessica is gone.*

"I *told* you," Eric's voice was a low growl as he frowned at the detective. "Piper isn't the one who is the threat. She's the one the bastard is after. And, yeah, I get that you have your techs, Layla, but we both know they are nowhere near my skill level. Give me access, and I can prove that Piper didn't send any emails to Grady. The real killer did. He lured the guy here, and then he murdered Grady—"

"Tortured him first," the detective corrected. "Tortured, then murdered."

Piper sucked in a breath. "Tortured?"

"Um." The detective's dark stare was watchful. "Your former lover was stabbed eleven times. That's a whole lot of rage." And her gaze slid to Eric, then Ben. "Know anyone who might be carrying around that kind of rage? That kind of jealousy?"

Okay, so what, now the cop was saying that Eric or Ben had committed the crime? "No." Piper's shoulders straightened as a cold fury filled her. Bad enough that the woman had been accusing her, but to turn on Eric and Ben? "Hell, no." Rage shook her words. "They didn't do this, so don't even suggest it. They are *helping* me. Some sick prick is out there, he broke into my house—two times—and the cops ignored me. He set my house on fire! He destroyed my artwork by pouring red paint on the canvases in my gallery—"

"Yeah, about that..." The detective opened a manila file that she'd brought into the room. "I just got a report back on the analysis from the crime scene at your gallery. I took the liberty of helping myself to the file, thinking it might help with my homicide case, and you know what? That wasn't just paint on your canvases. It was blood."

"*What?*"

"And I'm betting that blood will match up to Grady Fox. Because eleven stab wounds...that will sure generate a lot of pain and suffering and a whole lot of blood."

Don't pass out. Don't. She could feel icy pinpricks in her face. Why couldn't she just wake up from this nightmare?

"You sure you know those two so well?" The detective gestured to Ben and then to Eric. "You think they are your protectors, don't you?"

"I think they aren't insane madmen who would stab a person eleven times and then take his blood and pour it on my paintings." What in the hell? "Yeah, I feel pretty good saying that's not them."

The detective gave a faint smile. It didn't reach her eyes. "I thought I knew Eric pretty well, too. But then I found out that he likes to circumvent the PD. I guess you can never know someone well enough, hmm?"

Piper's temples were pounding. "I want to know more about Jessica's accident."

"Oh, you will. Her vehicle appears to have run off the road. Like I said, no one even noticed it at first. Luckily, some hikers finally found her. The cops on the scene thought it was just a tragic accident, but, obviously, in light all the things happening now, I'll be sure that a full investigation is conducted."

Eric leaned forward. "I want Grady's computer. Give me ten minutes. Hell, give me five. Let me see what I can uncover."

"That's against the rules, and I can't break the rules, not even for you." Detective Lopez hadn't given Piper her phone back. Instead, the detective had put it on the table close to her left hand.

"Piper is cooperating," Ben said, voice sharp and hard. "And all you're doing is accusing. You obviously see that she's a target. You have to realize the killer is focused on her."

"Tell that to Grady Fox's family. Sure seemed like the killer was focused on him."

Ben turned to glare at Eric. "This is the *'good'* cop you were telling me about? The *'thorough'* detective you mentioned to me so many times before?"

Eric had a romantic relationship with the detective. He'd *had* that relationship. Past tense. Definitely past. And Piper wasn't going to focus on that right then because she had a million other problems occurring. She let out a deep breath and asked Detective Lopez, "What can I say to make you believe I had nothing to do with Grady's death?"

The detective shrugged. "When was the last time you talked with him?"

"A few years ago. He texted me. Apologized. I accepted his apology."

Detective Lopez frowned. "Why did he apologize?"

Piper would not let her gaze dart to Ben. "Because he'd gotten jealous. Acted out. He thought I was involved with someone else during our time together. He was wrong."

Considering now, the detective's gaze slid to Ben. "Did Grady happen to take that jealousy of his out on anyone in particular? If he apologized, if he acted out, then that makes me think Grady acted out on *someone*."

Piper knew that if she revealed the details of that last encounter, the detective would just think Ben was a suspect. He wasn't.

Ben would never do something so horrible. Neither would Eric. She knew them both. She...*trusted* them both.

Holy hell, I do. She didn't just trust her best friend. She trusted Eric. Completely and totally. Surprised, her gaze flew to him.

And she tried to figure out when things had changed between them.

"*Eric?*" The detective's voice was surprised. "Eric was your lover back then, Piper?"

"Uh, no—" she began.

"*We're done.*" Ben rose to his feet. "Detective, you have zero evidence against my client. She gave you her phone—keep it. Run all of your checks on it. And when you're done, give it back and maybe give her an apology, too." He motioned toward Piper. "You aren't helping her. You're wasting time, and we don't have time to waste. A killer is out there, and my brother and his team need to get hunting."

Eric gave him a cold smile. "Well said, brother." He stood, and his fingers curled around Piper's elbow. Inclining his head to the detective, he told her, "We are done. I thought you'd help, Layla. It's obvious a sick fuck is loose on the streets. One who is locked on Piper. He killed her ex-lover, and we both know you're going to find evidence to show that Jessica Bromley's car was sabotaged. Anything else would be just a little too convenient, don't you think? This guy is on some kind of mission. He's eliminating the people in Piper's life—past and present—"

"If that is the case, then you and your brother should both be very careful." The detective had risen, too. Her face showed her tension. "From what I can see, you two are Piper's past *and* her present, so that would make you and Ben the targets. *If* this guy is eliminating people in her life."

No, they couldn't be targets. Fear nearly choked Piper.

"Where will you be?" the detective asked Piper.

"With me," Eric said instantly. "So if you want to have any other sit-downs, give me a call."

Ben grunted. "But we aren't going to be so nice next time."

The interrogation room door opened. A tall, handsome, African American man with a completely shaved head and wearing what had to be a thousand-dollar suit stood in the doorway. "I'm here for my client."

"Kendrick Shaw?" The detective didn't sound impressed. More like pissed.

He smiled. "The one and only."

"You're too late." She waved him away. "I'm already done for today." She grabbed her file and Piper's phone and headed for the door. But she paused to frown back at Piper. Seemed to hesitate. Then… "Be careful." She pulled a business card out of her pocket. "Take this."

Piper's fingers closed around the card. "Do you believe me?"

"I believe that some serious shit is going down in my town. I believe I have a dead body that I have to handle. *He* is my vic. He is my focus. I have to give him justice because that is my job as a homicide detective." She expelled a rough breath. "But I absolutely do believe that you're in danger. You need to watch yourself and the people around you, because I think this mess could get a whole lot worse before it gets any better."

***

"I didn't send the email." Piper's voice was quiet. They were in Eric's car, he was taking her the hell away from the crowded police station, and all he wanted to do was pull the vehicle over and haul her into his arms.

"I'm not lying to you," Piper added quickly. "I didn't reach out to Grady. Though, God, I wish I had right now. I wish I had been talking to him so he would have known that wasn't me asking him to come here. I didn't lure him to this city, and I never, *never* would have wanted him to be hurt or killed!"

He spared her a quick glance. Shit, she was crying. He saw her swipe away a tear on her cheek.

"I hate this. I hate the bastard doing this. Grady and Jessica. *Jessica is dead?* She was my friend!" Another hard swipe on her cheek. "Who is going to be next? And why? Dammit, why? I haven't led anyone on. I haven't played games or—"

"*None* of this is on you." His voice was low and hard. "Understand that, Piper. You didn't do anything to cause this shit. It's all on the SOB out there. He's doing this. He's hurting people. He's the one that has to be stopped and punished. People like this—they could be crazy. They could be sick. They could be cold-blooded killers. But their actions have nothing to do with their victims. *What he is doing has nothing to do with you or anything you've done.*" The last thing that Eric would let her do was blame herself.

The light changed. He pushed down on the gas.

He heard Piper pull in a ragged breath.

"The detective seemed to blame me," she mumbled.

His hold tightened on the wheel. *Tread carefully.* "She's hunting a killer. We can count on her to do her job. She isn't going to stop until she finds him. Layla is very determined. And she isn't going to be misled by false information. She was pushing you—" Harder than he fucking liked.

"But she will see the truth. Her vic is Grady, and she's focusing on him. Her investigation into his murder is going to lead her back to the perp that we're after."

"There's...something between you."

Tread —

"Or there was, right? I could see it, when she looked at you. The two of you were involved."

He couldn't read the emotion in those words. "A long time ago—and briefly. We realized we were far better as friends than we'd be as lovers." Mostly because he hadn't let her or any other woman close. His attention had always been elsewhere, and that sure as shit hadn't been fair to Layla.

"You didn't seem like good friends today."

A rough laugh escaped him. "Yeah, she was furious because I hadn't called her before I went to confront Grady. The fact that I went into an active crime scene had her seeing red." She wouldn't forgive that one anytime soon. "But I had to go inside. I had to make sure the perp wasn't there—or that a live victim wasn't in the place, too."

"He was tortured. That's what she said."

Dammit. "Yes."

"The guy who did this...do you think he'll hurt me, too?"

They'd left the busy roads and were heading toward his house. "I wouldn't let that happen."

Now it was her turn to laugh. A sad, husky laugh. "I know that you like to think you control the world, but you don't."

"I control more than you think." Eric glanced into his rear-view mirror, spotting the car tailing them. Julia and Rick were following his orders. Level six protection meant that eyes were going to be watching her as closely as possible. Julia and Rick would be staying nearby, looking for trouble, and when their shift was over, another team would be replacing them.

Grady had been tortured, and, no, the same fate was not going to happen to Piper. No way, not any freaking day.

Simon had stayed at the station, the better to keep an eye on Layla's investigation. Simon also had an in with the ME, so he'd be reporting to Eric as soon as he got the official report on Grady's murder.

Ben had gone back to his house—*after* Eric ordered the guy to head home. His brother had been looking dead on his feet. Murder wasn't exactly Ben's specialty. The guy was the charmer, the schmoozer. He never got his hands dirty, and truth be told, Eric didn't want his little brother even encountering any kind of violence. Sure as hell, he didn't want Ben at a scene like the one he'd witnessed that day.

"You try to protect everyone," Piper said, as if she'd just read his mind. "But who protects you?"

"I don't need protecting."

"You just told me that you ran in that house today because you thought the perp might still be there. A murderer. What if he'd turned on you?"

"I was armed. And I had Simon as a back-up."

"I don't want anything happening to you. Not because of me."

They were nearing his gate. He slowed the car. Turned to glance at her. "Keep talking like that, Piper, and I'll start to think that you care." The words were meant to be mocking, teasing. He wanted to take away a little of her fear and pain.

After a small pause, Piper said, "Of course, I care. I always have. Maybe that's been the problem."

"What?" He was gaping. Dammit. Eric managed to get out of his stupor and open the gate. It swung open, and he stomped down on the gas, braking right in the middle of the rounded drive that led to the main entrance of his home. He killed the engine and whirled toward her. "Say that again."

She unhooked her seatbelt. Angled toward him. "I *care* about you, Eric. You're not some stranger. I've always cared, even when you made me madder than hell. You hurt me, and I still cared. You enraged me, and I still cared."

That was promising. Very, very promising.

"I can't remember my life without you being in it. You've been there, whether in the shadows or in big, bright, infuriating color for as long as I can remember." She swallowed. "So, yes, I *care*, and I don't want anything to happen to you. I don't want to go to some crime scene and see yellow police tape and hear that *you* were the one inside. That you were tortured or that you were killed. Because…I need you in my life. I want you there."

He shook his head. An instinctive movement because there was no way Piper was telling this stuff to him. She couldn't be saying that she really, truly needed him.

But it was the wrong gesture. So wrong. So typical of him when he tried to communicate with Piper. She sucked in a sharp breath and her hand flew out toward the door. She shoved it open and ran for the house.

Oh, the hell, *no*. "Piper!" He tried to lunge after her, but, shit, he still had on his seatbelt, and the damn thing jerked him back. Cursing and snarling, he freed himself and hurried after her. He caught her just as she was heading up the steps. He spun her back around to face him.

"Just stop, Eric! Let me go! I'm trying to not make an ass of myself again by saying—"

"Say any fucking thing you want to me, baby. But listen to me first, okay? Please? I was shaking my head because I couldn't believe you were saying that shit to me. That you actually—hell, I *care* about you, too." Care, such a tame word. A ridiculously easy, tame word. One that didn't come close to explaining how he actually felt about her. "I...care." The word jammed in his throat. "I want you in my life. I need you there. And if something were to happen and you left my world, dammit, nothing would be same." He wouldn't be the same. Without her, Eric was pretty sure he'd crash and burn.

***

Ben unlocked his door, shuffled inside, and threw his coat onto the nearest chair. It had been one hell of a day. He pinched the bridge of his nose as he headed for the kitchen. His head was pounding, and he kept thinking about the fear he'd seen in Piper's eyes.

Grady was dead. Piper had covered for him, she hadn't told the detective that the last time they'd encountered Grady, Ben had been the one punching the guy. He was sure that little detail would have put him high up on the detective's suspect list.

He grabbed a water from the fridge, lifted it to his mouth and—

Why was the light on in his bedroom?

He froze. The bottle of water was cold in his hand. Slowly, Ben turned his head toward the bedroom. The door was partially shut, and light streamed from the opening.

He was sure he'd turned off the light in there. But…

He shoved the water back into the fridge. Shut the door, moving as quietly as he could. Maybe he was mistaken. Maybe he'd left the light on when he'd hurried out that morning. He'd been worried about Piper, and he'd hauled ass out of the place.

Maybe he had…

Or…maybe he hadn't.

Ben grabbed a long knife from the kitchen block, and he crept to his bedroom. His breath came quickly, in and out, as he advanced. He couldn't move as quietly as Eric, but he was a pretty close second. And while he might not have all of Eric's fighting skills, he was a second degree black belt. Their father had insisted they both learn Taekwondo when they'd been younger.

His father had thought self-defense was a necessary part of life. Eric had gone on to take all sorts of classes, but Ben had kept his focus on the style he loved the most.

"I don't want you to ever be the one to start something, but if someone comes at you, you have to be able to defend yourself." His father's words swept through his mind as Ben closed in on the bedroom door.

He pushed it open. The door gave a low creak.

And—

The room was empty. The bed still unmade, the light shining from overhead. Nothing seemed out of place. Nothing appeared to have been moved in any way.

The tension slid from his shoulders. He was just jumpy. The whole nightmare with Piper had gotten into his head. He had a security system. If someone had gotten inside, he would have known about it.

But Piper's system hadn't gone off.

The thought sent a surge of adrenaline pumping through him—right before he felt the rush of movement at his back. Something slammed into the back of his head, and Ben hurtled toward the floor. The knife slipped from his fingers.

"You don't fucking deserve her!"

CHAPTER THIRTEEN

Piper stood in Eric's study. The same study where they'd made love on the desk. Wait, no, that hadn't been making love. It had just been fucking. Wild sex. Eric wasn't in love with her.

Her arms locked around her stomach. Eric paced just a few feet away from her. He seemed uncharacteristically unnerved. Eric never got unnerved. Did he?

But he had been at a murder scene that day. He'd seen her ex, found her ex's body.

And now he was probably trying to figure out what words he should give to her. Her breath sighed out. "You don't need to think about how to handle me."

He stopped pacing. Frowned at her.

"I'm not expecting you to make some grand declaration to me." Jumping out of the car could have been an overreaction. Sue her. She was a wee bit stressed. She'd found out Grady had been tortured and that Jessica was dead. Being rational wasn't exactly possible every second. So, she'd flipped out. Piper had her control back, for the moment. "I was just trying to explain that…I like you, okay? You're not the big, bad jerk that I thought you were."

"Good to know." A rough growl. And he strode toward her.

Her shoulders stiffened. "Eric?"

"I am not trying to figure out how to handle you. I will *never* figure out how to handle you. Because you never say or do what I expect. Just one of the things I enjoy about you."

"You have…other things?"

His smile came, moving slowly across his face, making that sexy slash appear in his cheek. Who needed dimples? She was all about the slash. "I have a list," Eric assured her.

She wanted to know what was on that list. She wanted to keep talking to him. She wanted to do anything to keep her mind off the fact that a killer was out there.

I'm sorry, Grady. And Jessica — God, Jess!

Eric's head tilted as he studied her. "And you probably have a list, too. A list of the things I've always done to make you insane."

She shook her head. "I don't make lists." That would require more organization. She tended to wing it.

His hand lifted and slid over her cheek. "I'm glad that you need me. I'm fucking grateful as hell that you want me."

Her heart jerked. When he touched her, she could count on that quick leap. Maybe she *should* have been making a list all this time.

"I want you, Piper, and that desire didn't lessen because I had you in my bed. It just got stronger."

She felt the same way.

She just wished all of this had happened under different circumstances. Circumstances that didn't involve death and some psycho stalker.

"I need you, too, Piper."

She was inching toward him.

"I need you because you make me smile. You keep me on my toes. You make me laugh when I just want to be pissed at the world."

Her head tipped back and she wet her lips.

His gaze immediately settled on her mouth. That hadn't been her intention. Honestly. She was just nervous and her lips had gone dry.

"I'm a jealous bastard, Piper. You need to realize that. Especially when it comes to you, my emotions can be primitive."

Now she laughed. "And you think I don't get jealous?" What, was that supposed to be an emotion magically limited to men? Uh, no. "When I saw the way the detective was looking at you, when I realized that the two of you had been involved, I pretty much wanted to attack." But attacking a detective who was interrogating her? Bad plan. Very bad. She'd managed to keep her cool…and only lost her shit in the car. "I can be jealous and possessive, too. You should understand that, right now. I'm not the kind of lover who shares. It's me and only me."

"Why would I want anyone else?"

Okay, sometimes, he could say the most perfect, sweetest things. Sometimes.

Both of his hands cupped her jaw. He stared down at her, and she could see the desire in his eyes. Handsome, fierce Eric.

"I don't want anything to happen to you." Her words were husky and soft.

"My job is protection. It's what I do."

He was supposed to sit behind his fancy desk and come up with tech inventions to save the world. She didn't want him running into crime scenes, looking for perps. "What if you'd been the man who was wheeled out of that house? What if you'd been put in the body bag?" Piper had to blink because tears tried to fill her eyes again. "I can't have that. I won't. I—"

His phone rang. The loud, high-pitched peal filled the room.

"It's Ben," he muttered. "Give me just a second." Eric backed away as he pulled out his phone.

She sucked in a deep breath. She had almost crossed a major line there. Said something that she'd kept secret for a very long time.

He put the phone to his ear. "Hey, look, we're okay here. I got Piper home safe and sound and—"

His face changed. Went dark and lethal in a flash. It was almost as if she stared at a stranger.

"Who the fuck is this?" Eric demanded.

Piper took a step toward him as fear rushed through her blood.

"Where is my brother?" he snarled. "What the hell do you—" His gaze flew to Piper. "Ben's not the one fucking her."

The echo of her heartbeat pounded in Piper's ears like a drum.

"I'm the one doing that. I'm the one fucking Piper. You hunting her lover? You want her lover to pay? It's me. *Me*. Not Ben. He's never been her lover, so you stay the fuck away from him, you stay—" Eric's words ended in a snarl as he yanked the phone from his ear. "Bastard hung up!"

"Eric?"

He was already calling someone else. "Simon, you at the station? Hell, yes, I need you. I need you to get to my brother's place, *now*. The perp just called. He's got Ben. Get Layla and more cops and come in with guns freaking blazing because that is exactly what I'll be doing."

***

"Is it true?" The low hiss filled Ben's ears as he fought to stay conscious. The piece of shit had attacked him from behind. He'd slammed something big and heavy into the back of Ben's head, and when Ben had fallen, the guy had grabbed Ben's head and rammed his face into the floor over and over.

Ben suspected his nose was broken. He didn't much fucking care.

What he cared about was stopping the bastard behind him.

Ben had blacked out once. His head burned and bled, but he knew if he passed out again, it was over.

"Are you Piper's lover?"

He'd known her stalker had attacked him. There was even something about the guy's voice that was familiar to him. "N-no." He was her best friend. Her family.

"*Were* you?" Something sharp pressed against his back. The guy had a knife.

Wait. So do I. But he'd lost his knife when he first hit the floor. His fingers scrambled out, scraping across the wooden floor as he searched for his weapon. "No…"

The knife sliced into him, a white-hot pain that had him gasping.

"One."

One? One what?

"Is your brother her lover?"

Ben shook his head and his fingers touched—

The handle of my steak knife.

"Your brother said he was her lover." The attacker's blade bit into him again. This time, it sliced into his side. "Two."

Ben clenched his teeth.

"Why would he lie? Why would he—"

Ben used his last bit of strength to roll toward his attacker. He felt pain blaze across his side, but he ignored it. "He'd lie to fuck with you! *To protect me!*" Ben tried to yell those words even as he shoved up with his knife, aiming for the guy's chest.

The bastard had on a ski mask. A bulky black shirt and some kind of thick vest. Black pants. What did he think? He was some freaking ninja?

The guy let out a scream when Ben's knife flew at his chest, and the attacker jumped back.

Guess you don't like being the one who gets stabbed.

The fellow turned and ran, rushing though Ben's home. Ben shoved onto his knees, intending to go after the piece of crap. He even made it up to his feet. A full-on stand, even as blood dripped into his eyes. He lunged forward. "Stop!"

Then Ben fell face first onto the floor. But he kept his grip on his trusty steak knife this time. He kept the grip, even as he felt himself start to pass out.

***

"I have your brother. Tell Piper I'm killing her lover right now."

Those words had turned Eric's blood to ice. The voice had been grating, rasping, and the SOB had called from Ben's phone.

"He should never have touched her. Never have touched what was mine. Never have fucked — "

"Eric, does he really have Ben?"

They were racing to the scene, and he'd brought Piper with him. For all Eric knew, the guy could have been bluffing. Maybe it was a trick, one designed to take Eric away from Piper. To separate them. Until he could figure out what the hell was really happening, he intended to keep her close.

Julia and Rick were racing right behind him. "He called from Ben's phone." Could mean nothing. Could mean the guy had just swiped his brother's phone. But…

I thought I heard Ben in the background.

They rounded the final corner that would take him to Ben's place, and Eric could hear sirens. He'd told Simon to have the cops go in with guns blazing, and from the sound of things, they sure were. They were going in loud and hard. A swirl of bright lights illuminated the scene, flashing in front of Ben's condo building.

Uniforms were running toward the building. An ambulance had parked nearby. The back doors hung open.

Eric braked his car. The Benz came to a rough stop. "You stay with me, every second, got it?" He didn't give her time to respond before they raced from the car. Eric grabbed her hand, making sure he had her close. Rick joined them immediately, his face even harder than usual as the blue lights hit him. Julia hurried forward, and Simon—

He was already rushing *from* the building.

EMTs passed Simon as they hurried in with a stretcher.

Eric raced for his friend. "Simon!"

Simon's head whipped toward him.

And Eric realized something was on Simon's shirt. Something dark. The blue lights hit him and illuminated Simon for a moment. Dark and red. Blood?

"He's alive!" Simon ran down the steps. He shoved past some of the uniforms. "Did you hear me, Eric? Ben is alive."

Eric let go of Piper's hand and grabbed Simon's shoulders. "That's his blood?"

Simon winced. "He was stabbed, but he's going to be okay. You just have to stay calm for—"

Eric shoved him out of the way.

"You can't go in there! The EMTs have to bring him out!" Simon shoved Eric right back. "Stand down, man. He's *alive*. Did you hear me? He's alive!"

Eric's heart thundered in his chest. His desperate gaze swept the scene. Gawking neighbors. Fresh-faced cops. A terrified Piper.

Piper.

Rick was right beside her. And Julia's gaze was on the crowd, moving suspiciously from person to person. *She's looking for the perp.*

"He got away," Simon said, voice lower, more controlled. "Eric was conscious when I got to him—Detective Lopez and I were the first on the scene. The guy was trying to drag himself out of his bedroom and go after the perp. Ben said he managed to stab the guy. Hell, Ben still had a death grip on his kitchen steak knife when we burst in his place. From what we could tell, the perp had been gone only moments—"

The EMTs were back. And Ben was on the stretcher.

A gasp slipped from Piper as she hurried toward Ben. "Ben!"

His head turned toward her.

Jesus. Blood stained Ben's face. Poured from his nose. Definitely broken. And there was one hell of a gash on Ben's forehead. His shirt had been cut away by the EMTs and Eric could see the bandages on his side.

Ben reached a hand toward Piper. "You...okay?"

The EMTs didn't slow down. They rushed toward the waiting ambulance.

Eric and Piper ran after him.

The EMTs loaded Ben up in a flash. The siren screamed.

Ben groaned. "Got...away. So...sorry."

His brother was killing him. "You have nothing to be sorry for."

"We need to get him to the hospital, right away." The EMT closest to Ben—a young woman with close-cropped, black hair—threw Eric an impatient glare. "Back up."

His brother was hurt. He didn't want Ben going anywhere alone. "That's my brother."

"Then get your ass in here," the other EMT—a balding man with a thin beard and too-pale skin—muttered. "We got room for one."

Eric wanted to go with his brother. His job was to protect him, always had been. A guy was supposed to look out for his baby brother, wasn't he? But...fuck, he hadn't looked out for him. And he'd been keeping secrets. He'd lied to his brother time and again about Piper.

The female EMT demanded, "Hurry!"

Ben shook his head. His wild gaze swept the scene. "Piper? *Piper!*"

"Go with him," Eric told her. "I'll be right behind you."

She scrambled into the ambulance. Ben reached for her hand. Held tight. And seemed to immediately settle down.

Eric backed away. Someone shut one of the ambulance's rear doors. One, then the other. He watched the ambulance drive away, and he realized that two of the most important people in his world were in that vehicle.

No, his world *was* in that ambulance.

He was supposed to protect Ben and Piper. He was failing them both.

***

"Thought...we were lovers..." Ben's words were a weak rasp.

The EMTs were buzzing around him, tending his wounds, and getting an IV set up.

"That's why...came after..."

Oh, God. His words ended in a mumble, but Piper knew exactly what Ben had been about to say. The attacker had come after Ben because he thought Ben was her lover.

The same bastard had gone after her former lover Grady. Had *killed* Grady.

If Ben hadn't been able to fight back...

Her hand tightened around his. She and Eric had been looking at this all wrong. They'd been thinking her exes could be suspects. They weren't. They were potential victims. The men that she'd dated, the lovers that she'd had—*they* were in danger.

Eric was in danger. Because she could hear his voice in her head, clear as day. The words he'd told to Ben's attacker. *"I'm the one fucking Piper. You hunting her lover? You want her lover to pay? It's me. Me. Not Ben. He's never been her lover, so you stay the fuck away from him."*

Eric had put a giant target right on his own back.

CHAPTER FOURTEEN

"I feel like I've been hit by a truck." Ben's grousing voice filled the hospital room.

Piper tensed and jumped from her chair. She'd been waiting beside his bed, and at those grumbling words, she knew he was finally back with her. "Not a truck, just some asshole."

His eyes fluttered open. "Pipe?" An old nickname. He hadn't called her that since they were kids. "Why do you look like someone died?" Then his eyes widened. "Shit, am I dead?"

Her lips curved. "No, but you are heavily drugged. You've got stitches in your back and side, and the doc said you'd suffered a concussion."

His lips pursed. "That would explain the drum playing in my head." His words were still rasping.

She lost her smile. "He went after you."

Ben frowned at her.

"Do you remember what happened?" Her fingers slid carefully along his hand, making sure not to disturb the IV line.

"I…remember being at my place. The light was…on. In my bedroom."

She waited. She could see him struggling to gather his thoughts.

"I went in…someone hit me from behind." His left hand lifted, as if he'd touch the wound, but then he stilled. "I think he stabbed me."

Her heart squeezed.

"One." His voice had dropped even more. "Two…" His brow wrinkled.

"Uh, Ben? What are you doing?"

His gaze held hers. Some of the confusion was slowly clearing. "I think the bastard was counting as he stabbed me."

She pulled in a quick breath. "Did you see his face?" The cops had already come by—twice—because they wanted to know the answer to that question.

Ben shook his head. "Wore…ski mask. Didn't see a…a damn thing."

Her heart was racing.

"Cops…didn't get him?"

It was Piper's turn to shake her head. "No, he'd already gotten away before they arrived."

"Fuck." The machines around him began to beep faster as he shoved upright.

She grabbed for his shoulders. "Stop! You're going to hurt yourself!"

"*He* hurt me! Some freak wearing a ski mask." His breath panted out. "But I got him, too." His eyes gleamed. "Stabbed him."

"I'm sorry." The apology slipped from her.

The furrow between his brows deepened.

"He came after you because of me." And if Ben had been killed...no, no. She would not go down that road. Not today, not tomorrow, not ever.

Ben's breath heaved in and out.

There was a quick knock at the door. Her shoulders tensed as she looked to the right. The door opened, and Eric strode inside. When he saw that Ben was awake—and struggling to sit up—a broad grin stretched across his face.

In a flash, Eric was across the room. He leaned down and hugged his brother. "You scared the hell out of me."

Ben tried to hug him back. The IV line didn't offer him a wide range of motion.

A lump rose in Piper's throat. She could practically feel the love between the two men. Sure, they fought. Brothers did that. Family did that. But she'd never doubted the bond between Eric and Ben. And as she stared at them, as she looked at their dark heads and as she saw the similarities in their faces...

Same hard jaws. Same firm lips.

She realized...those two men—they were the men she loved.

The realization pierced her straight to her soul. For a moment, she couldn't move at all.

Ben...she loved Ben the way you love your best friend. Freely, happily. She could be silly and crazy or anything in between with Ben. There was never any pressure or judgment.

An easy, casual love that she'd had for as long as she could remember.

But Eric...Eric was something different. And though she'd tried to fight it, though she'd tried to deny her own feelings for a very, very long time...that love had been there. Almost as if it had been waiting in the shadows.

It had started when she was fifteen, and he kissed her while the rain pounded down on them. It had continued when he held her hand at her mother's funeral. When he'd stood up and clapped so loud and wolf-whistled and shouted her name so clearly at her graduation ceremony.

He'd tormented her, teased her, hurt her...

And still they'd come back together.

He'd been there for her, and she'd kind of known, deep in her heart, that he *would* always be there. She could count on Eric. And what she felt for him wasn't casual or silly. It wasn't easy.

It was terrifying and consuming and overwhelming. She wanted to run, she wanted to deny it, but she couldn't.

She could only stand rooted to the spot as she fully realized that she didn't just *love* Eric Wilde.

She was *in* love with him. And, maybe, just maybe, she'd been in love with him since she was fifteen years old.

"Piper?" Eric frowned at her. He'd moved to stand beside the bed, directly opposite of her. "You okay?"

No, her whole world was just doing a bit of realigning. "Fine." She had to get a grip. Right now, the focus was on Ben. Her gaze swung back to him.

And she found him staring at her, and damn if his frown didn't look a whole lot like his older brother's.

"What's going on?" Ben muttered. His gaze slid from her to Eric. "Bro?" Ben cleared his throat. "That guy...I swear, I remember him asking me some questions...about you. About Piper—"

Eric's shoulders straightened. "He attacked you because he thought you were involved with Piper. Maybe that's what Grady told him. Maybe the bastard tortured Grady until the guy gave him a name—the name of the man Piper was involved with. You told me that Grady suspected you two were more than friends."

Piper let out a slow breath.

"But he went after the wrong brother," Eric added grimly.

Silence.

No, there as a faint tick, tick, tick from the clock on the wall. A round clock with a big face and that ticking seemed to get louder and louder until—

"Want to run that shit by me again?" Ben demanded, voice even rougher than it had been a moment before.

Eric blew out a hard breath. "He went after the wrong brother."

Ben's gaze swung to her. She didn't blush. Didn't avoid his gaze. Just met his stare straight-on. This wasn't how she would have preferred to tell him. She *really* would have preferred for her best friend not to be in a hospital bed, recovering from stab wounds and a concussion. And a broken nose—he hadn't seemed to realize that his nose was bandaged up yet. She wasn't going to point out that particular bit of news to him. He'd always been a little bit vain about his perfectly straight nose. Eric's nose had gotten broken in a basketball game once. It had the smallest of bumps on the ridge. She'd never told Eric that she liked that little bump—

"Piper, you're sleeping with my brother?"

Ben looked…hurt. And that hurt her. Because she hadn't gotten involved with Eric to hurt Ben. She'd gotten involved with him because she'd never wanted anyone more. Her chin lifted. "Yes."

"Fuck." Now there was anger in Ben's voice. "For how long?" His gaze swung back to Eric. "You two have been lying to me? Hiding this shit? It's been going on forever, right, and I was just some dumbass in the dark? I was—"

"It *just* started," Piper cut in. "And you're not a dumbass. You're my best friend."

Now his stare was back on her. "Best friends don't keep secrets."

She'd kept this one. "It just started. And I'm sorry that you were hurt by that bastard out there, sorrier than I can say. I would never, ever want you to be hurt."

He growled.

"But I'm not sorry that I'm involved with Eric."

Eric's head whipped toward her.

"I wanted him for a long time, and when we got together — we *just* got together, in case you missed it when I said that before — it was because I wanted him and he wanted me."

Ben shook his head. "There are some lines that you don't cross."

Her heart was squeezing in her chest again. Ben was staring at her with anger and pain, and she'd done that. She'd known that he wouldn't like it if she slept with his brother. But knowing what could happen, being afraid of Ben's reaction, she'd made a choice.

I wanted Eric more.

The truth settled in her very soul. "I crossed the line. I chose to do it." This was on her. Her choice. No matter what bridges had been burned.

But it hurts. It hurts so much when Ben looks at me that way.

"Don't be mad at Piper," Eric snapped. "I went after her. I wanted her for years. I wanted her and I—"

"Give us some time alone, Piper." The machines were beeping in the background. Ben's gaze darted away from hers. "I want to talk with my brother."

Her stare flew to Eric.

"I want to talk with my brother." The machines were louder.

As if in response, a nurse bustled inside. "You're awake!" A pretty nurse with a coffee cream complexion and jet black hair hurried toward the bed. With a quick, no-nonsense style, she began checking Ben's vital signs.

Piper backed up. A muscle flexed in Ben's jaw. And his hand lifted to touch his face and he finally seemed to realize—

"Shit! That prick broke my nose!"

Piper winced.

The nurse gave a low hum. "I can't have you getting upset. You've been through an ordeal, and you need to rest." Her stare took in both Piper and Eric. "You're family? Only family should be in here now."

"*He* is," Ben cut in.

He might as well have just cut Piper right in the heart. She retreated another step. "I'm sorry you were hurt. By that guy out there…and by me. Very, very sorry." She turned on her heel.

Before she could reach the door, Eric was there. He blocked her path and his dark eyes blazed at her.

They blazed even more when she had to quickly blink away tears.

"Piper?"

She shook her head. "He wants to talk to you. I'll be in the hallway." She needed to get out of that room right then.

"Simon is out there. I'll have an agent staying round the clock to keep an eye on Ben." Eric still didn't get out of her way. His hands had balled into fists at his sides.

Since he wasn't moving, she slipped around him. Piper made sure to keep her shoulders back and her head up. And the first tear didn't slide down her cheek until the hospital room door closed behind her.

"Piper!" Simon's worried voice. "Is something wrong? Is Ben okay?"

No, he wasn't okay. She doubted things would be okay for him anytime soon. She swallowed. Turning from Simon so he wouldn't see her tears, she demanded, "Tell me everything you know about the bastard who did this."

***

Eric waited for the nurse to finish. She didn't rush, but took her time as she checked on Ben.

Ben was tense and angry beneath her ministrations, and his gaze kept whipping to Eric.

An eternity later, the nurse strolled from the room. "If you need me, just press the little red button." The door closed with a soft click.

Ben balled his bedsheet into his fists. "You had to sleep with Piper."

Actually, yes, he'd *had* to sleep with her. Having her had pretty much been more important than breathing. But he didn't think Ben wanted to hear that particular fact.

"The world is full of women," Ben gritted out. "And you took *my* Piper?"

The world *was* full of women. But... "There is only one Piper. She's not yours, and she's not mine. She's a woman who chooses for herself what she wants."

Bitter laughter. "And you think she wants you?"

He certainly wanted her.

"I've seen you with women. You never stay with them. It's fleeting. Everything is fleeting with you." Ben shook his head. "Piper isn't like that. Don't you see? She's scared. She's been scared ever since her dad left. She doesn't know what it is to be with someone that she can truly trust. She needs that, more than anything. She needs a lover that she can count on to be there."

"I will be there for her."

"You've *never* been there for any of your other lovers!" The machines gave a fast beep,

beep, beep. "I'm supposed to believe Piper is different? When you've made her life hell for so many years?"

Eric stalked toward the bed. "You're injured. You're hurting. And you're on a lot of drugs. So, I'm taking your anger, but be careful what you say—"

"Piper fucked you."

Eric locked his back teeth.

"She said it *just* happened. What—was it the first night you had her at your place?"

He didn't say a word.

"The second night? Hell, it was, right? The second. I can see it on your face. She just fell into your bed and—"

"Be careful what you say." His words were low and lethal. "Because this is Piper, and she matters to us both, and when you cool down, you don't want to regret the things you can't take back."

"Like you can't take back sleeping with *my* best friend! Mine, not yours! Dammit, Piper was never supposed to be yours. She's too fucking good for you!"

"Tell me something I don't know." Again, his voice was low.

Ben blinked.

"I thought you wanted Piper, Ben. I thought—for years—that the two of you would wind up together. So I stood back. I played the role of the dick—yeah, that shit was deliberate, because when you can't have the one thing you want most, then you need to push it away. You need to get that temptation gone."

Surprise flashed on Ben's face. "You…what?"

"I couldn't have her. I thought she was meant for you. That the two of you would stop playing your games and you'd get married, and one day, I'd have to see your kids." The pain knifed through him. "You know what? I knew I'd fucking love those kids because they were part of you and they were part of her and I—" He stopped, flattening his lips together. His heart pounded in a too-fast drum beat. "I waited. I made sure I didn't overstep. The person I wanted most was right in front of me, but I didn't so much as touch her, and I made sure she didn't want to touch me."

Or…at least…he'd tried. He'd been the dick, the asshole, over and over…and now he was trying his best to show Piper that he was more. That he could be so much more for her.

Only time was running out. A psycho was out there, a man who wanted to kill.

A man who was already at the edge. No, over the edge.

Eric forced his hands to unclench. "I waited. You and Piper didn't get together, and then, a few days ago, you called me to her house. A stalker was after her. She was in danger. I'd been waiting—waiting all that time…and I could lose her to some sick SOB? No, not happening. I was done waiting. I was done holding back. If you wanted her that way, you should have manned the hell up sooner." Eric gave a fierce shake of his head. "*I* should have stepped up sooner. You see, I don't care if it pisses you off. I don't care if you're furious at me. I want Piper. By the grace of God, she seems to want me, too. I intend to have her for as long as she'll let me."

Ben gaped at him.

Eric lifted his hand and pointed his index finger at his brother. "But you don't get to look at her like she's some kind of villain. You don't get to hurt her. You're mad, fine, be mad at me. Yell at me. Curse me. When you're back on your feet, you can even try to kick my ass. Fair warning, you'll fail. Because you always do. But you can try." His hand dropped. "But you can't take out any rage or hurt on her. I won't let you. I'll stand between her and any pain out there. I'll stand between her and…" He shrugged. "Everything."

"Why?" Ben's question seemed strangled.

Eric lifted his eyebrows. "You're a smart guy, bro. Graduated at the top of your law class. Don't you know the answer to that question?"

Ben shook his head. But his eyes said…yeah, he knew. "It's not just sex."

"It's Piper." That was all that needed to be said. "Watch your mouth and watch your eyes. Don't look at her with fury again. No one hurts her, not even you."

Ben's shoulders slumped. "I don't…dammit, I can barely think." His eyes squeezed shut.

Eric stared at his little brother. "You're going to be protected. I'll keep my guards on you. He won't get another chance to come at you."

Ben's eyes opened, and he gave a slow, negative shake of his head. "It's not me that he's...gonna want."

Piper.

"It's...you." Fear flashed in Ben's eyes. "He wanted to destroy her lover. It's not me. It's you. He—he knows that now. He'll be coming after *you.*"

Good. That was exactly what Eric wanted.

CHAPTER FIFTEEN

"One of Ben's neighbors saw the guy running away. He jumped on a motorcycle. The ride was abandoned later. It was listed as stolen about two weeks ago, and since the neighbor who saw the fellow said the perp was wearing gloves…" Simon sighed out a long breath. "I'm not exactly thinking we're going to find prints on the ride."

Piper made sure her tears were gone before she turned to face Simon. "What else did the neighbor say about the guy?"

"She said he was tall. Fit. That he rushed out, holding his gloved hand to his chest." He gave her a satisfied smile. "That would be because Ben stabbed the bastard. Thanks to Ben, it seems like it's gonna be pretty easy to narrow down our suspects. We just need to line up all of your exes and see which one of them is sporting a knife wound to the chest."

A nurse walked past them. He paused to frown at Simon.

"What?" Simon frowned right back at him.

She grabbed Simon's arm and pulled him to the side of the hallway. "My exes? You still think one of them did this?" One of her exes was *dead!*

"I think it, and so does Detective Lopez. She's rounding them up and questioning them all. And, hey, if it's not them, then they still get a head's up from the cops that they could be in danger."

In danger...just because they knew her.

His gaze had gone all cold and hard. "And if it *is* one of them, then the bastard will get nailed."

"I want to help. I want to be there." Her hold tightened on him. "Is she bringing them into interrogation? Can I go in, too?"

He blinked. "Uh, that's not how it usually works, and you might want to lighten the death grip before you cut off my circulation."

She didn't lighten her grip. "Then tell me how it works. Or better yet, let's change how it works. Because sitting back isn't working for me. What happened with my email? Did we find out who really sent the note to Grady?"

"I think Lopez is finally going to let Eric take a crack at your laptop. About damn time."

Okay, yes, that was something. That was good. That was *progress.*

The door to Ben's room opened behind her. She heard the very distinct swish sound, and her shoulders stiffened.

"*Piper.*" Eric's deep voice rumbled and chill bumps popped up on her body. "We need to talk."

Simon pried her fingers off his arm. "And I want to go inside and check on Ben." He gave a little salute to Eric. "Let me know when you're ready to head down to the station." Then he motioned toward a guy in a suit who waited just a few feet away. The guy had been trying—unsuccessfully—to blend into the white, hospital wall. "Maurice will keep an eye on Ben. He'll make sure no unwanted visitors get anywhere near your brother."

Piper was pretty sure she fell into the unwanted visitor category. Ben had almost looked at her as if he hated her. He'd never stared at her with so much fury before.

Simon hurried to the hospital room. He shoved the door open. "Ben, you look like shit."

The door closed.

Piper rocked onto the balls of her feet as Eric closed the distance between them. Her mouth seemed to go dry, and she didn't know what to say.

"I'm going to the station."

Okay. He knew what to say. Immediately, she nodded. "I'm coming with you."

"Piper—"

"Seriously? Do not argue with me. I'm coming with you. Ben doesn't want me here with him. That much is obvious." Obvious to everyone.

The faint lines near his mouth deepened. "Ben is floating on pain meds. He doesn't know what the hell he was saying."

Ben knew exactly what he'd said. "I know him, and I know when he needs space to cool down." She also didn't want to get flayed by his blue stare right then. "I have to do something. Simon was just telling me that you are going to get access to my computer."

He pulled out his phone. Scanned the texts there. "Yours and Grady's. Lopez worked some magic with her chief and I'm being pulled in as a consult. I'm supposed to assist the PD's tech team…" A pause. "While she's working interrogations."

"Yeah." She licked her lower lip. "Simon told me about those, too. All the more reason for me to be at the station."

He didn't look convinced. "If one of those guys is the perp, all the more reason for you to be far away from the station."

She closed the last bit of distance between them. Her hands rose to press to his chest. "I feel safer when I'm with you." That was the truth. She actually did. But she was also playing him, just a wee bit, because she was scared out of her mind. She wanted to stay close to him because she thought he was in danger. He'd waved a red flag at the freaking insane bull. He'd told the psycho out there that he was her lover.

Now Eric was the next target. And that was why she wasn't leaving Eric alone. She was staying close to him. She might not be some trained security expect. Not even semi-trained, but, dammit, she was going to do everything possible to keep him safe.

And that meant making sure he wasn't alone.

He took her hand in his. "Come on."

As he headed down the hospital corridor, she hurried to keep up with him. They slid into an elevator, and he pressed the button for the ground floor.

"I know what you're doing," Eric murmured.

"Riding in an elevator?"

His lips thinned. "I don't need you to watch out for me."

Her chin kicked up. "Did you ever think that I just need to watch you? I mean, you want to keep me safe."

"Security is my business. My life."

"And you're—" Wait, no, not the time for some big, dramatic confession. "You're important to me." She'd toned it down. Kept her cool. "I need to know you're safe. I heard what you told the guy on the phone." And she paused. "Was there…anything about his voice that stood out to you?"

"Not a damn thing. He was whispering. Deliberately disguising his voice when he spoke to me."

Now that had her stomach clenching. "If he was disguising his voice, then does that mean he thought you'd recognize it otherwise?"

"Maybe. Or maybe he's just a freak who likes to whisper." The elevator dinged, and the doors opened. They stepped into the parking garage. The cavernous interior had his voice echoing.

He surveyed the garage. She knew he was looking for potential threats. She was doing the exact same thing. She'd always tried to be careful. What woman didn't? Situational awareness was pretty much female survival 101. She always glanced around when she was in a parking garage or just a parking lot. She made note of where other people were. Made sure no one was lingering by her car. And she checked to see if anyone was paying too much attention to her. When she was alone, she approached her car with her keys at the ready, no fumbling with her bag because she didn't want to be caught unaware.

And she even knew some self-defense. It had been Eric who had taught her how to defend herself. Eric who'd been a growling but patient instructor because he'd insisted she learn to fight before she headed off to college. Because… *"Guys get handsy. So you have to know how to break their hands."*

He opened the passenger door for her. She slid inside, her body brushing lightly against his, and she heard the sharp inhale of his breath.

It was good to know that she had a powerful impact on him. Only fair, considering the way he could make her feel. She remained silent while he got in the car, and then they were driving out of the garage.

"I'm sorry Ben was pulled into this mess." Her hands twisted in her lap. When she'd ridden in the ambulance with Ben, she'd been absolutely terrified. She'd held tightly to his hand and seen the blood pouring from his nose. And the gash on his forehead had seemed huge.

"I'm sorry Ben hurt you." His gaze slanted toward her before immediately returning to the road. "He doesn't get to tell you who to see or who to sleep with."

"Guess the secret is out, huh?"

"I'm glad."

"I bet you don't keep a lot of things from your brother."

"I keep more than you realize from him. For example, he had no clue that I've been lusting after you since I was seventeen."

He'd been— "That long?" she mumbled.

"Probably longer, if you want the truth. And you have starred in one hell of a lot of fantasies for me."

He'd sure been in plenty of hers, too. But… "I don't want to put you at risk."

"Piper?"

"Being my lover—it's a lethal business right now. I think it would be better…" *Say it. Spit out the words.* She had to do this. "I think it would be better if we cooled things off. I don't need to stay at your place any longer. I can stay at a hotel."

"You're kidding me."

Uh, no. "I think it's a good idea. We need to cool down—"

His hands tightened around the steering wheel. "Cool is the last thing I'm feeling right now," he muttered.

Yes, she could see that. Tension practically poured from him and his locked jaw. "It's better this way."

"Not for me. The only thing that is *better* for me is to have you in my house and in my bed."

It was a little hard to breathe. Her heart was double-timing a rhythm. "It's *safer.* If we sleep separately — as in completely different locations — this guy might get the idea that we aren't together and—"

"Fuck that. Let's back up." His breath heaved. "You want to be away from me because you think it will *protect* me?"

"Yes."

"*Not* because you don't want me any longer?"

Not want him? "I've never wanted anyone as much as I want you." They should be clear about this. No games. No pretenses. She'd never been the *player* type. "I risked my lifelong friendship with Ben because I wanted you so much. This isn't some fleeting desire that will just vanish."

Her words had come out too fast and probably too high, but she was nervous. Scared. Scared of the stalker. Scared of losing Eric. Scared of someone else getting hurt. She pulled on her ear lobe.

"Good." A rumble of satisfaction came from him. "Because I can't imagine not wanting you."

She sucked in a breath. Let it out. Sucked in another. "Have I ever told you that when you say nice things, it makes me nervous?"

"It's because I spent too many years being an asshole. I want to make you forget that." The car stopped. He turned to look at her. "You are beautiful and smart and funny. You're the sexiest woman I've ever met, and I don't plan to let you go."

She didn't want to let him go, either. "You are handsome and smart, and I think you're funny when you don't mean to be."

His lips quirked.

"You are by far the sexiest man I've ever met, and you are an incredible lover."

His eyes gleamed…

"But I like you alive. I don't want to put any extra risk on you or shove danger toward you, so if it's better for me to be in a hotel—"

"It's not." Flat. Hard. "I've got this. My team *has* this. Hell, a team has been following us since we left the hospital's parking garage. I have them watching you always. If he comes at us, he will be stopped." Eric reached for her hand. "I'm not about to lose you."

Good because she didn't want to lose him. Not now. Not ever.

And that was another truth that was pretty terrifying.

***

His fingers flew over the keyboard. When Eric got in the zone, Piper realized that he was well and truly in the zone. They were at the police station, in one of the back rooms, and several of the PD's tech members were hovered around him. They barked questions at one another. And they drank coffee—a lot of it. Time had flown by. Morning had come, and the harsh light trickled through the nearby blinds.

She watched, she listened, and she wished that she was in the interrogation room with Detective Lopez. Earlier, she'd caught a glimpse of Mark as he arrived at the station. He'd been wearing a leather coat, a black t-shirt, and battered jeans. He'd smiled when he'd seen her—she'd been heading back from the vending machine area—but then Detective Lopez had pushed him toward interrogation.

Mark had lost his smile.

He's a suspect or a would-be victim. All because he had the misfortune to date her.

Her gaze darted to the door, and as if on cue, it swung open.

Detective Lopez stood there. Her eyebrows lowered over her narrowed eyes. "Any progress yet?"

Eric didn't glance up from the computers around him.

"You can't rush perfection," one of the techs muttered.

Lopez rolled her eyes — and then her gaze settled on Piper. "We need to talk."

Piper looked over her shoulder. No one was hiding back there. The detective meant her.

"You and me, Piper. Can you spare a few moments?"

Lopez's voice wasn't overly hostile. But Piper was still cautious. "Is this for another interrogation?"

"It's for us to clear the air."

Piper rose.

"*Piper.*"

She blinked. Eric had seemed completely consumed by his task a moment ago, but now he was on his feet and his attention was on her.

"Take a breath, Wilde," Lopez instructed him. "I'm only escorting her down the hallway — *in a police station* — so that we can talk privately. She'll have a detective at her side every moment."

Yes, but was that a good or a bad thing? "Do I need a lawyer?"

"No." Lopez's full lips pressed together. "I'm just trying to apologize, okay?"

Eric was still on his feet. Still waiting. Piper waved him back down and stepped closer to the detective. "Why apologize? You were just doing your job."

"Yeah." Lopez winced. "But I enjoyed doing it a little too much. Overzealousness is a flaw I'm working on." A shrug. "You coming with me?"

Piper nodded. She cast a quick glance at Eric. He was frowning, so she shooed him back to his job and followed Lopez out of the tech room. The hallway was empty. "Where's Mark?"

"Your ex is cooling his heels in interrogation. It's a technique I use." They rounded the corner. Passed a uniformed cop. Lopez pointed to a closed door. "When you make the perps wait, it puts them on edge. When they are on the edge, it's easier for me to come in from a point of control."

Piper thought about how long she'd waited in interrogation. "You used that trick on me."

"Guilty." Another turn, this time, to the right, and Lopez opened a door that led to a small, slightly cramped office. Light poured through the blinds of the lone window in the tight space. "I know, I know, it's not much, but I traded size for a view. I happen to like sunshine." She waved Piper inside.

Piper glanced around, noting the files stacked haphazardly. The half-empty coffee mugs. And the framed photo of a young girl.

Lopez followed her gaze. "That's my sister." A smile tilted her lips, one that came and went far too quickly. "She was murdered on her eighth birthday."

OhmyGod. "I'm so sorry."

A quick nod. "Me, too." Her fingers reached for the frame. Traced carefully around the wooden edges. Piper got the feeling that Lopez touched that photo—in the exact same, tender manner—quite often. "She's the reason I have this job. When you lose someone you love, you can either give in to the pain or you can let the rage take over." A shrug. "I tend to fall onto the side of rage, just so you know."

Uh…"I think rage looks good on you."

Lopez's hand fell away from the frame. "I see why he likes you so much. You are…unexpected, huh? One of those women who marches to the beat of her own drum?"

Now Piper had to blink. "Isn't that what *you* are?"

"Absolutely. Why be like everyone else? That'd just be boring. And anyone can be boring. I'd rather be ragey. Dangerous. Someone has to make the sick assholes out there pay for their crimes. I figure that someone might as well be me." She sat in her chair then motioned for Piper to take the other seat in the office.

Piper eased down. The chair wobbled beneath her, and she was about fifty percent certain the chair would break before she got back up.

"I came off tough yesterday because I hadn't ruled you out as a suspect. For all I knew, you just blinked those big eyes of yours, twirled your hair, and got Eric to think you were some innocent damsel who needed rescuing…while you were actually out, you know, torturing your ex and killing him."

Piper deliberately blinked her "big eyes" at the detective. Once. Twice. "I don't twirl my hair."

"Noted."

"And I did need Eric's help—I still do, unfortunately, though I don't like it. I don't like it because now he's in danger."

A considering nod. "Because he's sleeping with you."

"Yes." She wasn't going to pull any punches.

Lopez nodded. "We slept together."

Piper ground her back teeth together. "I'm *trying* to like you."

"It didn't mean anything to either of us. Sure, it was fun. But there wasn't an emotional connection. And I could walk away. I do that—I always plan to walk away." Her gaze darted to the frame. "You get hurt otherwise."

Piper's chest burned. For an instant, she thought of her parents. Of the way her mother had fallen so hard when her father left.

"I've talked to your exes," Lopez murmured, voice much softer now. "Seems you have a pattern similar to my own. You like to walk away, too." Now the detective was studying her with a knowing glint in her eyes. "You going to walk out on Eric when this is all done? When you don't need him anymore?"

Piper folded her hands in her lap. The chair wobbled. "I feel like you're interrogating me again."

"I am."

"It's not polite to interrogate friends."

"We're not friends."

True. "Because you still think I might be some dangerous femme fatale?" She blinked her "big eyes" again.

And the detective shrugged again. "Because I'm worried you'll hurt someone who *is* my friend. Eric's not just hard edges and a growling voice. And I saw him when he looked at you. Don't play a game that you don't mean."

Her lips parted.

"Just so you know, we've already completed cleared one ex that you have. Eric and his team did most of the legwork on that guy. Zane Clarke? He's in London right now. Been there for the last six months, and Eric found a line of witnesses to verify that fact. He's in the clear."

Her lips twisted. "Of course, that still leaves other suspects for us."

A hard knock pounded at the door. A moment later, a uniformed cop poked his head inside. "Your guy in Interrogation Two is shouting up a storm. Says that he's leaving. That you can't keep him here."

"It's true," Lopez agreed with a touch of disgust. "I can't." She rose. "Time to see if he's angry enough to talk...and to show me his chest. I asked when he first arrived, but your ex said no dice. Made me suspicious, you know?" She motioned to the cop. "Keep an eye on him. I'll be right there."

Piper rose, too.

Lopez tucked a loose strand of curly hair back into the little bun at the base of her head. "Your tattoo artist has a pretty dark past."

"Yes, Detective Lopez, I—"

"Layla. It's just Layla for you, okay?"

She nodded. "I know about his sister."

A grunt. "You know they never found her killer? I asked for her case file to be sent over. Should arrive soon." She squared her shoulders. "Heard that he hit the bottle hard after her death."

Now Piper swallowed. "I guess he chose pain instead of rage."

Sympathy flashed in Layla's eyes. "Pain will pull you down. It will break you. And when you lose everything else, it will be the only thing that *never* lets you go. It's a bitch I don't like. Better to not let anyone get close, huh? Better to not let the pain inside. Better to put up your wall and block everyone else from touching your heart."

They were a lot alike. Maybe too similar. But...

It's already too late for me. Because she'd put up her wall, *after* she let Ben inside. And now, Eric was close, too. If she were to lose them...

"Is there anything I should know about Mark? Anything I can use in the interrogation?"

"He loved his sister. Her death gutted him." She thought about Mark and his past. "Because of her, he's going to want to help. He won't hold back. You don't need to treat him like a perp. That isn't what he is."

But Layla only smiled. "Didn't you notice? I treat everyone that way. Part of my charm."

"I did notice," Piper confided.

Layla's smile lingered a moment. When it disappeared, she seemed to study Piper with a softer gaze. "You want to watch?"

"What?"

"The interrogation? You want to watch?"

Hell to the yes. "Simon said that was against the rules."

Another eye roll from Layla. "I make my own damn rules." She yanked open the door.

Piper hurried to follow her.

"Besides, I'll reveal that you're there. Things will be on the up-and-up." Layla paused in the corridor. "Mostly."

Um...

Layla turned back to her. "Before we go in there, I want you to know—full disclosure—there is someone that I'm having trouble locating."

"Who?"

"It's not an ex you had listed as a lover, but an artist you've been working with. Didn't you just get back from a trip to see some of Dante Fallon's work?"

"Yes—I mean, not immediately. I went about six weeks ago."

"Yeah, that's what your travel records showed. I wanted to talk to the guy. Looked like you spent the weekend with him—"

"I spent the weekend at a bed and breakfast in Savannah. *Not* in Dante's bed."

Lopez smirked. "Settle down. I thought maybe you hadn't wanted to reveal info about him to Eric."

"And why wouldn't I tell Eric about him?" She had—she'd told the team at Wilde Securities about Dante when they'd asked for a list of artists who worked with the gallery.

"Because maybe the guy is a recent lover and you didn't want Eric to know about him?"

"Dante has never been my lover."

"Okay then." She inclined her head. "I've been trying to contact the guy. Especially since your exes seem to be fair game for our perp."

"Dante is a client. Nothing more."

"He's a missing client." An exhale from Layla. "I asked the Savannah PD to visit his house. They said it appears to have been closed down for days. A neighbor said Dante had a habit of disappearing, though, of unplugging and going away to paint. That he'd been doing that for years."

"He's…eccentric."

"Let's hope that's all he is. Like I said, I wanted to give you fair warning." She tapped her chin. "After the interrogation, I'm gonna want to hear exactly *how* he's eccentric."

She thought of Dante. Of his nervous fingers and his eyes that could focus on images only he could see. The guy was quiet, shy, and he blushed when he talked about his work. "Dante wouldn't hurt a fly." She'd actually seen him capture a fly and release it from his studio.

Layla's expression didn't change. "I'm not talking about flies. I'm talking about people."

CHAPTER SIXTEEN

Layla shut the interrogation room door with a soft click.

Mark tensed as he sat at the interrogation room table. "That sure took long enough!" His hands slapped against the top of the table. "Look, I'm here because of Piper. I want to know that she's all right."

Layla nodded. "Oh, she's definitely all right." She waved her hand toward the one-way mirror on the right wall. "In fact, she's very close. She's in there now, watching you."

And, on the other side of the one-way mirror, Piper winced.

Immediately, Mark's gaze swung toward her. Or, rather, to the mirror. "Piper?" He jumped to his feet and stumbled toward the mirror.

Piper swore he seemed to be staring straight at her.

"She can hear me? See me?"

"Definitely." Layla was brisk. "Now, can we get down to business?"

But Mark kept staring at the mirror. "Why is she in there?"

"Because she wanted to hear what you had to say. I want to hear, too. Shall we get things moving?" Impatience bit in her words.

Mark scraped a hand over his jaw. "Heard about what happened to that other guy—Grady. Saw it on the news."

"Did you know Grady Fox?"

"No, never met him. I knew his name, though. Piper mentioned him a few times." He kept staring at the mirror.

"We believe that it's possible someone could be targeting men who were involved with Piper Lane."

He didn't blink. "Is that why I'm at the station? You're warning me I could be in danger?"

"One of the reasons."

His nostrils flared. A small movement that told of his tension.

"Benjamin Wilde was attacked last night at his home."

"Ben?" Mark whipped around to face Layla.

Piper eased out the breath that she'd been holding. Mark and Ben had met a few times, even gone out for drinks. They'd gotten along, laughed. Mark had almost convinced Ben to get a tat…

"Is he okay?" Mark demanded.

"I guess that attack didn't make the news, hmmm?"

His hands fisted. "Is he okay?"

"He's recovering in the hospital. He has a broken nose, a concussion, and stab wounds. I don't think *okay* is the right word, but he's going to make it."

"Thank Christ."

"He was able to fight off his attacker. Able to even stab him with a kitchen knife." Her gaze slid over Mark. "We believe that Ben's attacker has a knife wound to his chest area."

"That's why you wanted to know if I'd show an officer my upper chest when I arrived?"

"Um." Very non-committal.

"You think I'm the guy who attacked him? You think *I* stabbed Ben?" He swung back to face the one-way mirror. "Is that what you think, Piper? You think I would do this?"

Piper pressed her lips together. A cop was in the room with her, and she could feel his stare on her.

"It's easy enough to clear up," Layla told Mark in a clear, crisp voice. "Just take off your shirt. Totally voluntary, of course. I don't have any sort of official power right now to demand that you remove your clothing. It's just, you know, a way to speed along the investigation. You *want* to help, don't you? I'm sure you do. If you don't want to show me, I can get a male officer in here to—"

He shrugged out of his coat. Stalked across the room and shoved it down on the table top.

Then he reached for the bottom of his t-shirt. He yanked it up.

There was a white bandage on his chest.

Piper lost her breath.

"Want to explain?" Layla rose to her feet. Her body was tense, her gaze cold.

He slowly peeled off the bandage. "I got new ink. Fresh as can fucking be." A blood-red rose was circled by angry thorns. "I kept it covered for a bit. No one stabbed me. I didn't attack Ben. I didn't kill Grady. And I *don't* like being a suspect." His gaze didn't return to the one-way mirror. Piper could practically feel his rage. "I'm done here. I thought I was at the station to help, not to be your lead suspect." He hauled his shirt back on. Shoved the bandage into the pocket of his coat before he scooped up the coat and headed for—

"You are helping," Layla assured him. "Now you're one less name on my list. I can move on with my investigation. Not waste time on leads that don't pan out. I have a victim down in the morgue. I want to give him justice. Justice is important, don't you think?"

His hold tightened on the jacket. "Damn straight. People should always get what they deserve."

She nodded. "Your sister didn't get justice."

He fired a furious glance her way. "What do you know about my sister? Did Piper tell you—"

Layla held up her hand. "I know your sister was murdered and that her killer was never caught. I know it must have been incredibly painful for you, and I'm very sorry for your loss."

He gave a bitter laugh. "People say 'I'm sorry' all the time. Doesn't mean jack." He began to pace. "The detectives on her case gave up by the second week. The second freaking week! Acted like she didn't matter. They should have kept searching."

"I don't give up easily." She advanced toward him as Piper watched. "I work until I catch my killer."

Another laugh. "You always catch them? I don't buy it. No one—"

"I don't always catch them. But I don't give up. I don't forget the cases. I keep working them. *I work until I catch my killer.*"

He licked his lower lip. "You really mean that?"

She nodded. "I am asking you…is there anything else you need to tell me about Piper Lane? About anyone you may have seen around her shop? Anyone who was paying extra attention to Piper's assistant, Jessica—"

"Jessica?" A line appeared between his eyes. "No one asked me about her before." His lips pursed. "She came to my shop one day last week. Or maybe two weeks ago? Not sure. She wanted a new tat."

Piper found herself leaning toward the glass.

"What kind of tat?" Layla asked.

"A wolf. A big, black wolf. Told me she wanted something beautiful and savage. And she even sent me a pic..." He fumbled in his back pocket and pulled out a phone.

Piper whirled toward the cop who'd been silently watching with her. "I need to see that picture." Adrenaline poured through her.

But the fresh-faced guy shook his head. "No, you're supposed to stay here, not go inside."

"I *need* to see that picture." Because she thought she knew the wolf. Or rather, the artist who'd made the wolf. She stopped asking for permission—especially since it looked as if she wasn't getting that permission. She just ran past the cop. He shouted after her, but she didn't stop. She yanked open the door to the interrogation room and hurried inside.

Layla glanced up, and her eyes flared in alarm. "Piper—"

"*It's Dante Fallon's work.*" The description of the wolf—God, Jessica had described it with those exact words the first time she'd seen the painting of what Dante called his "Dark Wolf."

Jessica. A pang shot through Piper.

Mark remained silent as Layla turned the phone toward Piper. The image staring back at her— "Dante." She nodded. "I would know his work anywhere."

"She never got the tat," Mark muttered. "She called the next day, sounding pissed. Told me she'd broken up with her boyfriend, and she was over that shit. Told me wolves didn't mate for life. Said they were just assholes like everyone else."

Her boyfriend? Piper met Layla's stare.

"Dante," Mark repeated the name softly. "I remember him. Skulky kind of guy. Would never stare you straight in the eyes for long. Came in my shop once or twice. Told me some BS about looking for inspiration."

Layla still gripped the phone. "Piper, did your assistant show a special interest in Dante Fallon?"

"She took him out to lunch a few times when he came to the area. He didn't know the town, and she said she wanted to help him." Had they been romantic? "Jessica dates a lot of guys. She likes to have fun and—"

"Dated," Layla cut through her words. "She *dated* them. She *liked* to have fun. She's gone, Piper."

Piper pressed a hand to her heart. Her heart seemed to burn.

"She's gone, and Dante Fallon is missing," Layla said.

Mark pulled his phone from Layla's hand. "Go find him. Get him to show you his damn chest." His gaze pinned Piper. "You should have known it wasn't me."

Her hand fell to her side. "I'm sorry that you've been pulled into this mess."

"I thought you knew me. That I knew you." Mark shook his head. "But you were just in there watching me and thinking I was some criminal?" He shouldered past her. "I'm done here."

She started to hurry after him.

Layla touched her shoulder. "Let him go. Our focus needs to be on Dante Fallon."

Piper shook off the detective and marched out after Mark. She caught up to him in the hallway. "You could be a target. You have to be on guard. Maybe we can get a police officer to—"

Mark whirled toward her. "I don't need cops shadowing my movements. You really think the people who visit my shop want to pass a cop on their way in? Way to kill the fun vibe of the place." He shook his head. "I'll be on guard. I know how to take care of myself. If that asshole comes my way, I'll deal with him." Then he blew out a hard breath. "I'm sorry I exploded on you, okay? This shit—it's a mess, and you're in the middle of it." His lips twisted. "And where is *your* protection? I thought that your bodyguard was supposed to be staying close at all times, but I don't see him."

"That's because I'm behind you," Eric announced.

Mark's shoulders stiffened.

"But thanks for the concern," Eric added, voice sounding everything but thankful.

Mark's eyes remained on Piper. "You need me, you know where to find me." His lips thinned. "And next time, don't send the cops after me. Come to me yourself." He spun on his heel and stormed away.

Layla gave a low whistle as she joined Piper in the hallway. "That man has a lot of anger bubbling up inside."

"Do you blame him?" Piper asked.

"No, but I'm betting my anger can beat his any day."

Eric glanced back and forth between them. "I'm guessing Mark checked out?"

"Yeah," Layla responded. "He's got a shiny new tat on his chest—really nice, detailed work, by the way, I might have to see him for my next piece—but no stab wound. He's clear."

"I've got someone you might want to check out," Eric announced, tension evident in his body. "Because I was able to track down the person who really sent that email to Grady. Sure, the fellow tapped into Piper's email address, but he didn't do it from anywhere near here. In fact, the guy was located in Savannah, and I believe it was—"

"Dante Fallon?" Piper supplied.

Eric frowned at her.

Layla patted his shoulder. "You're a little late to the party. Come in my office, and we'll bring you up to speed."

***

"I remember him." Eric's fingers tightened on the neck of the beer bottle in his hand. They were back at his house—finally back, after one hell of a day. The cops in Savannah and Atlanta—and all points in between—were searching for Dante Fallon. His face had been flashed to the media, and the public had learned that the guy was a person of interest in a murder investigation.

Layla was confident that he'd be found by dawn.

Eric had his own staff members looking for the guy. He had access to every credit card the fellow possessed. His team was looking for Dante's digital footprint. If the cops didn't find him, Wilde Securities would.

He took a swig of the beer. "He was at the gallery the day I came to install your security system there." He could have sent a junior tech over to do the job, but he'd wanted to go himself. After all, it was Piper. "Nervous guy with long hair that kept falling into his eyes. He wanted to take you to lunch." Shit, the scene was so clear in his head. "I told him to fuck off because we were working."

She sat on the couch, clad in a pair of yoga pants and a loose top. Her legs were curled under her. She looked small and delicate and heartbreakingly sexy. "Jessica took him to lunch that day. It was the first time she went out with him." Piper had a glass of wine in her hand. As he watched, she lifted the wine to her lips. Only

Piper didn't sip the wine. She chugged it, draining that glass and then setting it down, a bit too hard, on the nearby table. "Dammit, that was the day she started talking so much about him. About how different he was." She hauled the back of her hand over her cheek.

She's crying. And there wasn't a damn thing he could do to make her stop crying. He wished he could take away all of her pain.

"She was my friend, not just my assistant. She had a great laugh and all these dreams. These plans. She wanted to go to art school. She wanted to paint in Paris. She wanted to fall in love." Another hard swipe over Piper's cheek. "Jessica thought he was a good guy, you know? I thought the same thing. How can someone be like that? How can a man fool so many people? How can he fool a lover?"

Eric put down his beer. He strode toward her and eased onto the couch at her side. "Some people are very good at lying."

"Jessica is dead. Grady is dead. And Ben is recovering in the hospital." She bit her lip. "I don't think this guy is just good at lying. I think he's good at killing." She squeezed her eyes shut. "Why? Why is Dante doing this? And why get close to Jessica if he was just going to kill her?"

"Because getting close to her allowed him access to you. She probably gave him your email password. She gave him your schedule. She told him things about you that he wanted to know."

Her eyes opened. He could see the tears glistening in her stare.

"And he just started killing?" Piper asked softly. "Just woke up one day and decided he'd kill Jessica and my ex?"

"There could have been some sort of trigger that pushed him over the edge. Something that severed his control, and after that, he was lost. Or..." But Eric stopped.

Piper leaned toward him. "No, you don't get to stop. You don't get to just say 'or' and have your voice trail off. *Tell me.*"

"Or this isn't his first time." The option that Eric favored. "You aren't the first woman he stalked. There is a history of behavior like this for him. If he did it before, then he got away with it before. He learned from any mistakes he made. In other words, we're dealing with a killer who has a real taste for this sort of thing."

Her lower lip trembled. "Ben said...it was like the guy was counting when he stabbed him."

And Grady had been stabbed eleven times. He'd need to do a search, find out what other unsolved crimes between Atlanta and Savannah might involve a victim who'd been stabbed eleven times. Maybe he'd turn up nothing.

Or maybe not.

"Do you want some more wine?" He reached for her glass. "I'll get you some."

"I don't want to get drunk. That doesn't help. If I drink too much, I'll just be drunk and crying, and that's a hot mess you don't want to face right now."

He put the glass back down and caged her with his arms on the couch. "I don't think you're a hot mess."

"Then you are not looking at me right." She glanced up at the ceiling, and he knew she was trying to stop her tears. "I'm a mess. Jessica is dead, my best friend is in the hospital and currently hating me, and I want to run out of this house and track down Dante. I want to find him. I want to hunt the streets until he turns up, and then I want to stop him." Her voice grew hushed. "I don't usually want to hurt anyone. But I want to hurt him."

He studied her. "You still remember the self-defense moves I taught you?"

Now her gaze flew to his. "As if I could forget them. You drilled them into me. Threw me on the mat so often that—"

He winced. "You were going to college. I wanted you safe. I wasn't going to be there to watch over you every day."

"Oh, please. You didn't watch over me in high school. You…" Her eyes widened. "Wait, did you?"

He had to kiss her. Had to brush his lips over hers. "If I'd had my way, I would have protected you from every pain that you've ever felt." But people didn't get to live in bubbles. And the world could be a dark and cruel place.

"You think I don't feel the same way about you?" She surprised him by asking. "You think I don't want to protect you, too? You've got a target on you. And that's one of the main reasons I want to find this guy. I want to stop Dante before he can hurt you. I *can't* let him hurt you."

Eric stood up. Caught her hand and pulled Piper to her feet, too. "Let's see if you still have it."

"It?" She looked doubtful.

"You used to be able to throw me. I want to make sure you still can. Let's practice some of your defense moves—"

"Do you think he'll get to me?"

Only over my dead body. "It pays to be careful." Eric was going to make sure she was as safe as possible.

"You dragged me to all of those Krav Maga classes," she murmured. "Did I ever say thank you?"

He'd studied all sorts of martial arts while growing up, and when it came time to make sure that Piper could protect herself, he'd brought her to the gym for Krav Maga. Krav Maga was constantly developing, and it had seemed to be the perfect defense for her. Designed to be learned quickly, she was able to pick up some fast and vicious techniques. "I want to see what you've still got. Let's start with the straight punch."

"I don't want to hurt you."

Eric shrugged. "If you hurt me, then I'm just not moving fast enough." He smiled at her. "Don't hold back on me. Show me everything you've got."

Her gaze searched his. "You think he's going to get to me."

"I think I want to make sure that if I'm not at your side, you kick the guy's ass." He rolled back his shoulders. He was in sweats and a t-shirt. There was plenty of room in the study, and there was no time like the present. "Show me."

She shrugged and drove a powerful front punch at him.

Damn nice.

"Where's the best place to hit with that punch?" Eric demanded as he dodged.

"Eyes, nose, or throat."

Wherever the attacker was most vulnerable. They circled each other. He liked that her body stayed poised to fight, that she rocked on the balls of her feet. As they sparred, she came at him with a quick knee kick, then one going for his groin.

He smiled at her. He'd rather see her fighting instead of crying any day. "You've kept up your practice."

One shoulder rolled. "I might have even learned a few new tricks."

He feigned walking away, acting as if they were done, only to spin back and grab her arm. She responded perfectly. Piper didn't try to jerk back or fight his hold by pulling against him.

Instead, she used his own force to strengthen herself as she propelled toward him and delivered a fast, hard kick.

Damn but she was amazing and sexy.

But she frowned at him. "Did I hurt you?"

"*Never* apologize when an asshole grabs you."

He went at her again, and this time, because she was hesitating, he was able to take her down. He used care — because this was fucking Piper. Being on the floor was an incredibly vulnerable position and he closed in, moving quickly to see how she would react.

She used his distance against him. *Perfect.* She watched him with wide eyes and then she kicked out at him, catching him and taking his ass down, too. Piper leapt to her feet, and he smiled. *Rule one, baby. Always get up as fast as you can. Get up and run away.*

He jumped back to his feet. "What are the five targets you always aim for?"

"Eyes, nose, throat, groin, or a knee."

Eric nodded approvingly.

She turned away.

Then he rushed toward her. In Krav Maga, they hadn't worked on flipping an attacker, but he'd taught her some extra techniques back in the day.

He grabbed her from behind. Immediately, she moved to throw off his balance. Her butt shoved back at him as he stumbled and she grabbed his arm, using his own momentum to send him hurtling to the floor.

He stayed there, a smile curving his lips.

Then she climbed on top of him. "I won." Piper sat over his hips, the soft fabric of her yoga pants brushing against his groin. Her knees sank into the carpet on either side of his body.

No, baby, I won. Because you are fucking perfect.

Piper leaned forward and rested her hands on his chest. "I should have thanked you back then, but I just thought you were being a controlling asshole."

Eric winced. "I am a controlling asshole."

"You're more than that." She brushed her lips over his. "Sometimes, I think you're a white knight."

Not even close. He was sure Ben didn't think of him that way.

But she kissed him again. A soft, tender kiss.

"Gonna want a whole lot more than that," he warned her. Piper had to feel the growing arousal shoving against her. Having her that close was the worst kind of temptation. Or maybe the best. She pretty much just had to freaking breathe for him to get turned on so…

"How much more?" Piper whispered as her head rose, and she stared into his eyes.

"Everything." An absolute truth.

She smiled at him. She didn't get that he was dead serious. This wasn't some game for him. No casual fuck. This was Piper, and he wanted everything.

Would he be able to settle for just pieces of her? The parts that she'd give him? No promise of forever because she was afraid of being hurt?

Her finger rose and lightly traced over his lips. "You look so serious." Her hand trailed over to caress his jaw, sliding against the stubble there.

He needed her to understand… "I've hurt you in the past, but I will never hurt you again. You can trust me."

"I do trust you." She sat straight up again, pushing the crotch of her yoga pants down against him with a little wiggle. As he watched, she lifted off her shirt and tossed it to the side. She wore a sexy, white bra, one that did this cute little crisscross thing in the front. But she unhooked it fast, and he didn't get to admire the lacy bra for long.

He was too busy admiring her gorgeous breasts. Her nipples were tight, and they thrust toward him. He started to drool. A bit.

"The clothes need to go," Piper murmured, and then she was pushing up his shirt. Her fingers—cool and soft—were roving over his abs. His chest.

And his cock just got harder.

She smiled at him.

Her words echoed through his head again. *I do trust you.* "How…long?"

"I need the first one to be fast," she murmured. "Because I really want you—"

Because she...*Dear God,* she was going to break him. He rolled them, a quick turn of their bodies, but made sure to cushion her. Piper slid beneath him. He braced his arms on either side of her head, and his legs pushed between hers. "How long have you trusted me?"

Her eyes widened. "I don't know. It's just...there. I'd trust you with my life."

Good, baby. Because you are my life. A thought that was an absolute truth.

He kissed her. Kissed her hard. A fierce and wild kiss. Eric thrust his tongue into her mouth and savored her. And as he kissed her, his hand slid down her body. He caught the soft fabric of her yoga pants and shoved them down. She helped him, arching her hips and kicking out of the pants and her panties. Soon, she was naked beneath him. Wonderfully, perfectly naked.

And when a man saw a woman bared that way for him...

He had to taste. He had to lick. He had to freaking worship.

He started with her breasts. Licked and sucked her nipples. Made her moan and shiver. He loved it when her nails scraped over his shoulders. Loved it when she called out his name. Down, down he went, pushing apart her thighs even more, lightly blowing over her exposed sex before he put his mouth on her. Her hips rocked hard against him, and she probably would have lunged off the carpet if he hadn't clamped his hands down around her hips. He held her tightly, making sure he got all of the time he needed—and that she came. He felt her orgasm building as her body tensed. Her breath panted out, and with every lick and stroke, she pushed against his mouth. Wanting more.

So he gave her more. He gave and gave until she screamed his name.

He prepared to drive into her, he prepared to—

She had him on his back in a blink. Piper pinned his arms to the lush carpeting. "Not so fast."

She was incredible.

She bent her head. Pressed her mouth to his throat. Licked. Kissed. Sucked the skin.

A growl broke from him. Piper just laughed. Then she sat up and started hauling off his shirt. He was more than happy to help. They nearly ripped the thing before they got it off. Her fingers slid over his chest. Her sexy little tongue stroked his nipple, and his hands clenched at his sides. He didn't know how long his control was going to last. Not with her mouth on him. Not with her mouth slowly kissing a path down his stomach and—

Oh, fuck. She tugged at the top of his jogging pants. He wasn't wearing underwear, and when she tugged the pants down, his eager cock sprang toward her. Her touch was like silk against him as she stroked him from root to tip, again and again. He figured she wanted to drive him absolutely out of his frigging mind. Good. Because she was succeeding.

She put her mouth on him. Those red lips. That soft tongue. She took his cock into her mouth, and Eric *knew* he was a goner. Lost. His hips arched against her, and he kissed his control good-bye.

He wanted her too much, and her mouth felt like the best paradise in the world. But he was about to come, and he damn well wanted her to come with him.

He pulled her up.

"Eric!"

He lifted her easily, holding her hips so that she straddled him. With one long, deep thrust, his cock pushed into her core—wet, tight, hot.

Perfect.

Her head tipped back. Her thighs squeezed his hips.

Using his hold on her, Eric raised her up and brought her down, over and over, sliding balls deep and retreating. Then his right hand moved to stroke her clit. He watched her because she was such a thing of beauty when she came. The most gorgeous woman he'd ever seen as—

"Eric!"

He was such a goner. He rolled her beneath him. Grabbed her legs, draped them over his shoulder, and pounded into her. Control was history. There was only her. The hot grip of her body and the sweet sound of her moans. The softness of her skin.

He erupted into her, coming on a wave of pleasure that wiped him out. Gutted him. And he held her close. He kissed her. Kept thrusting. Kept wanting and wanting even as he came. Kept wanting…her.

As he always had.

As he always would.

And after, he slowly lowered her legs. His fingers slid along her ankle, and he pressed a soft kiss to her sexy little half moon tat.

***

Piper cracked open one eyelid. "You're carrying me."

"Because you're out cold."

"No." A yawn. "I'm awake."

He just tightened his hold on her. He was carrying her up the stairs. That was all strong and romantic and sexy. She snuggled a little closer to him. "You make me feel safe."

True.

"And you make me feel complete," Eric told her in his low, deep voice.

His words caught her by surprise. Wait, had he really said that? She was in a heavy sleep fog and—

"Relax, Piper. I've got you."

They were at the top of the stairs. He turned and took her into his room. Put her carefully down on the bed and eased her beneath the covers.

He climbed in beside her. It was the most natural thing in the world for her to turn toward him and slide closer. To put her hand over his beating heart. And as sleep pulled at her, she heard herself whisper, "I've got *you*."

CHAPTER SEVENTEEN

The gallery had a new alarm system. All fancy with bells and whistles. Was he supposed to be impressed? Intimidated?

Eric Wilde and his employees thought they were the only people in the world who could string up some tech.

Wrong.

He disabled the system, sure, it took a little longer than he would have liked, and there were a few moments when he started to sweat, but he got inside.

Thanks to Jessica, he knew a whole lot about the security there, and Eric's team had been a little sloppy—they should have started fresh with a whole new system, not just done upgrades.

Their mistake.

Maybe they'd been rushed. He could give them the benefit of the doubt. After all, the cops had taken their time doing their crime scene BS. The Wilde Securities team had only been able to work their magic after the cops had finally cleared out.

Maybe they planned to do more at the gallery. Too bad they weren't going to have that opportunity.

He slipped inside. Took a deep breath. Could have sworn that he smelled Piper in there. That sweet scent that she liked. Lavender.

He took out his knife. Slid his finger over the blade.

It was time for the final act. Time for the big show. No more waiting. Whistling, he stepped forward. And he brought along his surprise…

***

The sharp ringing woke Eric. He jerked upright, his heart racing, even as his hand flew toward his nightstand. His fingers closed around his phone, and he yanked it toward him.

Gallery breach. One of the sensors at Piper's gallery had just gone off. The main security detail team on the gallery would be notified immediately, and the system would also send an automatic alert to the Atlanta PD. The sensor wasn't connected to the main system at her place, but it had been a back-up that he'd ordered installed. Just in case the perp somehow got inside her gallery again…

And he had.

"What's happening?" Piper's worried voice.

"Someone is in your gallery."

Someone who didn't realize that he'd just been caught. The cops would go in fast and quietly, as would the security team. They'd trap the bastard. They'd—

A call came through on his phone. He frowned at the number even as he answered it. "Wilde—"

"It's Mark Rogue. Someone is at the gallery!" Mark's voice was frantic. "I see them, man! I see them! The lights are on and someone is on the second floor—up in Piper's work area."

"The cops are coming—so are my team members." Eric had given his card and number to Mark after they'd talked at the gallery. He'd told Mark to call him if the guy ever saw anything suspicious. "You stay where you are, understand?"

"No, man, *no*. This is the bastard who's been tormenting Piper! He's not getting away! Not like the sonofabitch who killed my sister. It's not gonna happen again, you understand me? I won't let him get away again!"

"No, just listen, Mark—"

But the guy had hung up. So much for listening.

Piper jumped from the bed. "Someone is at my gallery?"

"The cops are on the way, so are my team members—"

"So are we! You're not leaving me behind. We're going—*come on!*"

***

"You sonofabitch!" Mark raised the gun he'd taken from his shop. The gun that he kept locked beneath the counter because a guy could never be too careful. The gun felt heavy and cold in his hand, and his fingers were shaking. "Why did you do this? Why did you do this to her?"

Dante Fallon looked up at him, eyes wide, and blood still coming from a wound on his chest. The guy had a knife gripped in his fingers, and he lunged—

Mark's fingers squeezed the trigger. Just squeezed and squeezed, and Dante jerked back. It looked like he tried to speak, but if he said something, Mark couldn't hear him over the thunder of the gunfire. He just kept squeezing, Dante kept jerking, and then...

Nothing.

Dante was on the floor. Blood was all around him. Blood had spread to some of the easels nearby. Dante's chest rose and fell and a wheezing came from him—

Footsteps thundered up the stairs. *"Freeze!"* A woman's voice yelled. Then, immediately, *"Drop the gun!"*

Was he supposed to freeze? Or drop the gun? For a moment, Mark wasn't sure. He only knew that he'd...

He'd shot a man.

Dante stopped wheezing.

His chest stopped rising and falling.

I killed a man.

"Drop the gun, Mark!" The shout came from the woman. *"Now!"*

He dropped the gun and, in the next moment, hard hands grabbed him. His arms were pulled behind his back, and he felt metal snap around his wrists. *Handcuffs.*

Then he was staring into a woman's dark, deep eyes. A woman he knew. Detective Lopez.

"What did you do?" she whispered.

"He had a knife. He was going to stab me." Mark licked his lips. "I couldn't let him get away. Katie's killer got away. Did you know that?" His voice was rising and falling. To him, it sounded a touch insane.

What must it sound like to the cops?

"Her killer got away." His voice rose even more. "I couldn't let it happen again. It couldn't happen again. Tell Piper, tell her—" But he broke off because uniformed cops were shoving him toward the stairs.

He looked back and saw that the detective had dropped to her knees next to Dante.

"I've got a knife here!" Detective Lopez called out. "Bag it and tag it!"

As he strained to peer over his shoulder, Mark saw her put her fingers to Dante's neck.

How many bullets had he fired into the guy? It had all passed in a blur. A terrible, thundering blur.

Dante was gone. Dead. And Mark had done it. At least the guy wouldn't hurt Piper again. Or anyone. He was—

"Pulse!" Detective Lopez yelled. "Get an EMT in here, now!" She pointed at Mark. "Keep him secure!"

He struggled against the guards who held him. "He can't hurt her! He can't hurt her again!"

Sympathy flashed in the detective's pretty eyes. "I'll make sure he doesn't. Don't fight them, okay? We have procedures to follow." Then, voice roughening, she ordered, "Get him outside!" It looked like she was applying pressure to Dante's wounds. Blood was covering her fingers...

The uniforms hauled Mark downstairs. Cops were everywhere, and he saw that some of Eric's security people were there, too. Two men and a woman—all in suits. The cops were keeping them back. Blue lights flashed in a sickening blur as Mark was led toward a patrol car.

"Am I being arrested?" His question was dazed.

"You have the right to remain silent..." One of the uniforms began.

Another car roared to the scene. A fancy Benz. He knew it was Eric even before the guy braked and jumped out of the car. And Piper was there, too. She tried to rush to Mark, but Eric caught her arms and pulled her against him.

The cops guided Mark toward a patrol car. "I shot him!" Mark yelled out.

Was he supposed to stay silent? The cops had said…

Eric and Piper came closer. Eric kept a tight hold on Piper.

Mark tried to smile at Piper, but he was honestly scared as shit. Was he being arrested? He'd just… "He came at me with a knife. I had to defend myself."

But it wasn't just about defending himself. He'd known, even before he went inside the gallery, that he was going to kill Dante.

Piper's face was too pale. Eric looked pissed. Probably mad because he hadn't been the one to save the day.

This time…this time…*I saved the day.*

The cops pushed him into the back seat of the patrol car. And he probably should have smiled at Piper, but Mark felt his shoulders hunch as the door slammed shut.

Is he dead?

Through the window, he saw an ambulance barrel down the road. Its screaming siren hurt his ears, and it barely seemed to come to a full stop before a man and woman jumped from the back of the vehicle and raced toward the gallery. He turned his head and watched them. Watched in silence as the siren kept screaming and the lights kept flashing.

Moments later, they were back. Dante was on the stretcher. The female EMT was pounding on his chest as she ran with him and then helped load the guy in the ambulance.

Doors slammed.

The ambulance roared away.

Alive or dead?

Did it matter? Mark had done his job. His gaze slid to the right. Piper was staring at him. She'd been watching him the whole time. Once more, he tried to smile, but he couldn't.

CHAPTER EIGHTEEN

Piper paced the hospital's emergency room waiting area, the gleaming tile bright beneath her feet. The waiting room was packed—something she found crazy for two AM. To the right, a woman held a bloody cloth over a gash in her arm. An older man coughed hard into his fist as a nurse steered him to the back, and a young boy held his right arm carefully to his chest, tears trickling down his cheeks. There were plenty of other people there, hunched over as they filled out intake forms, and there were nervous relatives waiting in the lobby as they worried about—

Layla shoved open the doors to the OR. She marched toward Piper and Eric, and Piper could easily see the blood on the woman's shirt. As Layla approached, Piper found herself holding her breath.

Layla gave a hard shake of her head. "He didn't make it. Died on the table."

A woman to the right flinched. The little boy cried harder.

Piper grabbed Layla's arm and steered her away from the kid—and the people who were listening too intently. Eric was right beside them. Tension rolled off his body.

"I had questions for him," Layla snapped. Her frustration was palpable. "I wanted to talk to the guy. He wasn't supposed to get the easy way out."

Death was easy? Since when?

They huddled in the corridor, and as the bright overhead light fell on Layla's face, Piper could see the strain the other woman felt. It was obvious in her eyes and in the faint lines around her lips.

"What's going to happen to Mark?" Piper asked quietly.

Layla sighed. "He's being held at the station. I have plenty of questions for him, too. Like, why the hell did guy run into the gallery instead of calling the police?"

"He called me," Eric replied quietly. "I told him to stand the fuck down, but I guess with his history, with his sister, he couldn't just sit back."

Piper frowned at Eric.

He exhaled slowly. "I learned all about her when I was running a background check on him. My team members said her death gutted him."

"Mark couldn't let another killer get away." Layla straightened her shoulders. "I have to grill him. I have to learn every single thing that happened in the gallery." Another hard exhale.

"If it's clear self-defense, no charges will be filed, but that's not a decision that will be reached quickly. We'll have to conduct a full investigation. I'll need to get reports from the crime scene techs. I'll need any security footage that's available. Hell, I'll need everything I can get my hands on." Her phone gave a little ding and vibrated on her hip. She pulled it out and scanned the text. "Well, this is a start, and it certainly makes things easier." She looked up at Piper. "From the Savannah PD. They just found a storage locker that belonged to Dante. Got lots of paintings inside—including several of you." A pause. "They also found women's underwear in there. Could be yours. Could be someone else's. We'll be finding out, though."

God.

"Go home," Layla urged her. "I've got one hell of a long night in front of me, but for you two…" Now her gaze darted to Eric, as well. "It could finally be over. Dante is dead, and he won't be hurting anyone else. Mark made sure of that."

Another brisk nod, and she walked away. Layla pulled out her phone and talked briskly to her contact. Her voice faded as she rounded the corridor.

Piper felt rooted to the spot. Was it over?

"What in the hell…?" Eric began.

Her gaze swung to him. But he wasn't looking at her. He was looking at the elevator that had just opened. At the man—garbed in a paper hospital gown and rolling an IV stand with him—who was slowly shuffling out of the elevator even as a nurse tried to steady him.

"Ben?" Eric rushed toward him. "What in the hell are you doing?"

"Coming to see you." Ben was a little pale. Correction, a lot pale. And he still had a big, white bandage across his nose. "Both of you."

"He's not following orders," the nurse groused. "Trying to tear out stitches and get his dumb self hurt, that's what he's doing."

Piper bit her lip, not wanting to get closer and feel the force of Ben's fury again. Eric hurried to slide an arm around Ben and help steady him.

Ben inclined his head to the nurse. "She told me…you were down here. That there'd been a shooting…"

The nurse—the same pretty woman with the close-cropped, dark hair that they'd met the other day—glared at him. "I told you they were *fine*. That they hadn't been injured. I never expected you to get all tornado crazy and fly out of your room after them!"

"We *are* fine," Eric assured him quietly as he tried to steer Ben back to the elevator. "You're the one down here with your ass hanging out."

And he was. When Ben turned, he completely flashed Piper.

"Is it…safe?" Ben asked haltingly. "Is Piper okay?" Now he glanced over his shoulder at her.

There wasn't fury in his gaze. No hurt, either. Just worry.

She pressed her lips together. She was so sick of crying. Piper forced herself to give a strong nod. "Okay."

Ben tried to pull away from Eric, but Eric just held him tighter. "I'm sorry, Piper," Ben burst out. "I'm a jackass, and you know it. Hell, you know it better than others."

"We all know it," the nurse pointed out flatly.

He ignored her.

"I want my best friend," Ben mumbled. "I want you to always be there for me, and I am a selfish bastard because I didn't think about what you need. What you want."

It wasn't true. He did always encourage her to go after what she wanted.

Except in this particular instance...

"You want him." His gaze swung to a glowering Eric. "Then take him. And he'd better be damn grateful for every single day that he gets to spend with you."

"You think I don't know that shit?" Eric demanded immediately. "Are you still high on the pain meds? Of course, I need to be fucking grateful. Piper is the best thing that ever happened to me, and, yes, I *know* it."

"Good," Ben threw back. "Because she's my best friend, and you'd better treat her right."

Piper stumbled forward. She threw her arms around them and wound up hugging both Ben and Eric and the IV line. "I love you," the words just came from her.

But she wasn't just talking to Ben.

I love you, Eric. She had to tell him. If the threat was gone, if they were free and clear, then maybe…maybe giving her heart to a lover wasn't a risk, after all.

Maybe Eric could be the lover that she finally counted on.

"This is…interesting," the nurse said. "Are you all a couple?"

Piper pulled back. She stared at the two men who meant so much to her—but in different ways.

"We're family," Ben said firmly.

Piper smiled. Yes, they were.

A faint grin lifted Eric's lips. "And we're getting his crazy ass back upstairs."

"Good." Ben gave an approving nod. "Because I think my knees are about to buckle. Bro, catch me if I fall."

***

"I hate to just leave Mark in jail," Piper said as she slumped back in Eric's car. "I mean, he was trying to help me. Trying to stop Dante!"

"I've already called Kendrick Shaw. He'll be at the station with Mark by now." Eric cranked his Benz. "Don't worry, Mark won't be alone.

Layla isn't about to railroad him. She'll find the truth. She always does."

Weariness pulled at him. If Mark had just stayed back, Eric's team could have contained Dante. The cops could have taken him in to custody. But the night had ended in more bloodshed. More death.

"Did Dante have a stab wound?" Piper asked quietly. "In his chest? I mean, that's what we were looking for, right? Because Ben was able to stab his attacker…"

Eric had been able to get the answer to this question at the gallery. "One of the cops told me that he did."

A low sigh. "Then that's the end, isn't it? The proof we needed? Everything is over. Layla just has to release Mark, and then life can go back to normal."

Eric didn't want things to go back to the way they'd been. He wanted better. He wanted different. He wanted her.

He'd had Piper in his home and in his bed. Finally, really, truly in his life, and he didn't want to let her go.

So how was he going to convince her to stay?

***

"You're my lawyer?" Mark frowned at the slick guy beside him. A fellow that practically oozed cash in a suit that smelled of money. "Since when?"

"Since Eric Wilde hired me." The guy flashed him a million-dollar smile. "My name is Kendrick Shaw, and I am not only the best criminal defense attorney in Atlanta, but I'm the best on the whole East Coast."

Uh, okay. The guy was definitely confident.

Kendrick straightened his already straight suit. "Now let me do most of the talking when the cops come in. The less you say, the better it is."

"I *killed* Dante—"

"Jesus, see, that's why I just told you…*the less you say, the better it is.*" Kendrick puffed out his cheeks. "You acted in self-defense that's what you did. There was no *killing* involved. You saw a break-in at your friend's gallery."

Mark nodded. "I knew someone was inside."

"You called Eric Wilde to alert him." Kendrick's eyes were hard. "That's what Wilde told me."

Mark gave another nod. "I wanted him to know what was happening."

Kendrick's hands motioned vaguely in the air. Sort of an I-Need-More gesture. When Mark didn't add more, Kendrick said, "*And* because you were afraid the perp would get away. That's why you rushed inside. You didn't want him to get away, so you went into the gallery."

"The front door was open," Mark mumbled. His temples were pounding, and his chest ached.

The new tattoo seemed to burn his skin. "The lights were on upstairs, so I ran up there."

"When you found Dante Fallon—"

"He had a knife, he lunged at me, so I killed—" Mark stopped and corrected himself. "So I acted in self-defense."

The lawyer nodded approvingly. "Damn straight you did." He rubbed his hands together. "I'll have you back at your home before the sun rises."

***

She opened her eyes and stared up at the ceiling. Sunlight trickled through the blinds. A new day.

Eric's arm was thrown across her stomach, as if he'd wanted to hold her in sleep. It was the second time she'd woken to find him still holding her, and she liked it. Before, she really hadn't ever slept well with her lovers. She'd been restless, far too aware of every single movement they made during the night, but with Eric, it was different.

He was different. Her head turned so that she could stare at him. Tousled hair. Long, black lashes. Dark stubble on his hard jaw. In sleep, he didn't look vulnerable or softer in any way. He just still looked sexy and fierce, and Piper found herself inching closer to him.

She pressed a kiss to his jaw. "Thank you," she whispered.

His eyes didn't open. "I think every day should start this way." His voice held no grogginess, but was completely awake and aware.

A smile curved her lips. "With me thanking you?"

"No." Now his eyes opened. So deep and dark and consuming. "With you in bed with me. With you beside me."

Her heart gave a fast flutter. "You're wanting this…us…to continue?"

"No."

No? She pulled away from him, clutching the sheet to her chest as she sat up in bed. A fast, jerky movement.

"I've lied to you, Piper."

A horrible cold slid through her. She was in his bed, she'd woken feeling all happy and safe, and now she feared her world was about to implode. Talk about one brutal wake-up. "What lie?"

He sat up, slowly. The sheet pooled at his waist, and his powerful abs flexed. "There is something you need to know about me. Something that I've hidden from you for a very long time." He scrubbed a hand over his stubble-covered jaw. "This shit is hard because I've never done it before."

Never done what before? Told a lover to kiss off? That was exactly what she felt like he was doing. The case was over and he was already kicking her out? No, no, this could not be happening. She'd let him in. She'd trusted him. She'd started to think of a future with him.

Why in the hell would you ever do that? A cold voice from inside chided her. *You know he isn't looking for forever. There is no forever. Not with a lover, there is just—*

"Come back to me."

Piper blinked. Stared hard at him. She should get out of the bed. Get dressed. Not have this conversation when her only covering was a sheet.

He took her right hand in his and pried it away from the sheet. Her left still clutched the black silk to her chest.

His face was so serious. So intense.

"I wish I'd gone back to you after the first kiss."

The first kiss?

"I don't want only sex from you. I never wanted that. I want *you*. All of you." His hold tightened on her hand. "I'm in love with you, Piper Lane, and I have been, for a very long time."

She shook her head.

His jaw hardened even more. "I know you think I'm a jerk. Give me a chance to show you that I can be more. That we might be able to have more together." Then he let her go. Let her hand fall from his. "I understand that you don't feel the same way. I'm not trying to pressure you for anything. I just wanted you to know—you're important to me, baby. You always have been.

You always will be. Whatever decision you make about us, I'll respect it." He swallowed. "I wanted to say the words, you know? Because all this time, when you thought I didn't care or that I was just the biggest asshole in the world, the truth is that *all this time,* I loved you."

Her heart was drumming out of control. Absolute madness. Chaos to the extreme. "Say it again."

He frowned. A sexy little furrow between his brows. "I'm the biggest asshole in the world—"

She tackled him. Smashed the sheet between their bodies and tumbled him back onto the bed. "That part is fun, but say you love me again."

He smiled. Flashed her that slash, and some of the intensity in his eyes changed to pure heat. "I love you, Piper Lane."

She kissed him. Laughed. Kissed him again. And felt joy pour through her.

His arms wrapped around her hips. "Does this mean you don't mind?"

"Mind?" Piper rose up, her knees pushing down on either side of his hips. The sheet fell and she didn't care. "I love you, Eric."

He tensed beneath her. Piper felt his whole body go rock hard. "You don't need to say—"

"I absolutely, one hundred percent need to say these words." She stared into his eyes. And he stared into her eyes. Impressive—his gaze didn't drop to her bare breasts. He looked her dead in the eyes as she told him, "I love you. At first, it was a teenage crush, and then I was so mad at you. Mad for a long time. No one could ever drive me as crazy as you do…but, Eric, you aren't the biggest asshole in the world. You can be so sweet and caring and protective. You can make me smile, and you can give me so much pleasure. With you, I start to think about the future, and I've never done that, not with anyone else."

His muscles seemed to relax.

"I want to try a relationship with you." Maybe they'd crash and burn but…she didn't think so. She thought they just might work.

The whole happy ending thing. A life together. Holding hands. Building dreams. Maybe even a family…one day.

A little girl with his eyes would be incredible.

"Piper, I want to try everything with you." He winked. "And I don't just mean sexually, baby."

A laugh spilled from her. God, she was *happy*. After everything that had happened, it seemed so foreign to feel this way.

"When I think of my future, you're there, Piper. Every step of the way. At my side. My partner, with me." His hands slid over her hips. "I want to marry you. But, shit, that's not me trying to make you feel pressured."

Her eyes widened.

"It's just me wanting you. Wanting to offer you anything and everything in this world. Just know that, okay? I love you, and I want to marry you. But if you don't want that, screw it. After what happened with your parents…" He shook his head. "Give me only what you want to give. If you don't ever want to get married, that's fine. We can be together any way you want. Because being with you is what makes me happy."

Her eyes were starting to burn. She blinked quickly even as her smile grew. Perhaps it was time to stop being afraid of the future. Long past time. She wasn't her mother. And Eric definitely wasn't like her father.

They were different. Their path could be different. Their ending could be different.

Happy. Good.

"Let's take it one day at a time," he told her, voice rasping. She could feel his heavy erection pushing against her, and Piper rubbed her sex over him. He groaned. "One, uh, day…at a time. We'll go as fast or—*God, that feels good*—as slow as you want."

Piper's tongue swiped over her lower lip. "I don't want to go slow." Her whole life felt as if it had been lived in slow motion. And after everything that had happened—Jessica and Grady's death, Ben's horrible injuries, Dante…No, life wasn't meant to be taken *slowly*. It was meant to be lived. You should grab every single moment, hold tight, and go wild. Experience everything—joy, fear, and love. *Live*. No holding back. "I want you. So…yes."

"Yes?" His face went slack with shock.

"Yes."

He let out a shout and hauled her down toward him. His mouth met hers in a wild, delirious kiss. They were both laughing and smiling and kissing, and she was so happy.

So incredibly happy.

She had a lover she trusted. A man who knew all of her secrets. A man who was ready to stand by her no matter what threats came.

A man who wouldn't leave when the going got tough. A man who wanted her, who loved her—and she loved him just as fiercely.

When he thrust into her, she moaned and he growled out her name. He drove deep and hard, and her hips lifted eagerly toward him. He was what she wanted—the man she'd always crave.

Her nails raked over his arms as she urged him to go faster, even harder. His hand slid between their bodies, and he stroked her clit, caressing her even as his hips pistoned against her. He filled her completely, and her body was so sensitive, so tuned to him.

He kissed her, and she loved the feel of his mouth against hers. The man knew how to kiss. He knew how to caress her and how to give her the best pleasure.

He made certain that she came first. And she sure did. Piper's orgasm slammed through her. Toe-curlingly awesome. So strong that she screamed as her whole body stiffened.

Then he came. He pushed deep inside of her and let go. He shuddered against her, and she could have sworn that she tasted the pleasure in his kiss.

Or maybe…maybe that was love.

When her head lifted, Piper smiled at him.

CHAPTER NINETEEN

"I need to see Mark today," Piper announced as she stood in Eric's kitchen.

He lifted a mug of coffee to his lips, but a frown hardened his gaze. "He left the station. No charges were filed." That didn't mean charges *wouldn't* be filed. The investigation was still ongoing, that was what Layla had texted to Eric. But the lawyer representing Mark had made sure that the guy was able to walk out of the station before dawn.

With Kendrick Shaw, you got what you paid for.

"May I borrow your phone?" She gave a little wince. "I need to get a new one or maybe Layla will return mine soon."

He slid the phone toward her.

She flashed him one of her sunny smiles as she tapped in a number and then put the phone to her ear.

She loves me. The knowledge was still sinking in. And he was almost afraid to believe it. The idea that he might get Piper, that he could have everything he'd ever wanted…it was a little scary. He was afraid that something would happen. Something would go wrong. Because no one got a happy ending, right? That didn't work in real life.

Just in books.

"Mark? It's Piper." A pause. "Yes, I'm using Eric's phone because the cops still have mine. Listen, I just—I wanted to check on you. Make sure you're okay."

He'd killed a man. Eric doubted that the guy was okay.

"You're at the shop already?" Surprise had her eyes flaring as she looked over at Eric. "Yes, I'll come see you. All right. Yes, I—um…" She frowned down at the phone.

Eric eased closer to her. "Everything okay?"

She handed him back the phone. Bit her lip. "He's already back at the tattoo shop. Said he can see the crime scene team coming and going from the gallery." She tucked a lock of hair behind her ear. Tugged on the lobe. "He sounded funny. Stressed, but I guess that's to be expected, isn't it? After everything that happened?"

"Yes."

She swallowed. "He wants me to come and see him. Said he had something that he needed to tell me." Her breath blew out. "I'm going to run by and then I'm supposed to go meet the insurance adjustor at my house so that we can get started on the repairs." She hopped off the barstool. "I need to—"

His fingers closed around her wrist. "Stop."

Her head tipped back and she looked up at him.

"I love you."

The shadows immediately left her eyes. She smiled at him. "I love you, too."

Good. Wanted to make sure that hadn't just been one awesome-ass dream. He kissed her. "You don't have to do all that stuff alone. I can go with you. I can—"

"The bad guy is dead, remember? I don't need twenty-four seven protection any longer. It's all clear. Call off the level six protection because I am good to go."

So it would seem. He kissed her again. "How about this…I'd like to go with you. Because I enjoy being with you. And I'm still scared as shit because of everything that happened. It would make me feel so much better if I could tag along with you." He flashed what he hoped was a charming smile.

She frowned suspiciously at him.

He kicked the smile up a notch. "I'm also really, really good with insurance adjustors."

Piper gave a light laugh. God, he loved that sound.

"Fine," she relented. "But I figured you'd have more important things to do today."

"Nothing is more important than you."

Her lips parted. Her gaze searched his. "You say that like you mean it."

He absolutely did mean it. "I'll get the keys."

***

Layla Lopez was on her fourth cup of coffee. Fourth, maybe fifth? She'd kinda lost count because she'd pulled an all-nighter.

A sharp knock sounded at her office door. She grunted a response, and the door opened, revealing her partner Mac's rumpled form.

"Pack it in, woman." A big, brown envelope was tucked under his right arm. "The bad guy is on a slab. There is no reason for you to be dead on your feet."

He was right. She should go home. Collapse in bed. Stop drinking the coffee that tasted like piss. She stretched her shoulders and heard weird things pop. But as she rose, her gaze was drawn to the envelope. "What's that?"

He looked down. "Oh, yeah. The report on Mark Rogue's sister. Poor girl never stood a chance. She was hit from behind and then stabbed by her assailant." He shuffled forward and offered the file to her. "No wonder he went all crazy on the perp last night. That shit happened to my sister, and I'd be forgetting my badge, too."

She exhaled. "Thanks, Mac."

He pointed at her, one short and stubby finger. "Go home. Get some rest. Don't let this job kill you." He turned on his heels. "The perps aren't worth it."

She put the envelope down on her desk. He was right. The case was done. The killer was on a slab.

Her fingers slid over the envelope…

***

Piper's gaze swept toward the gallery. Sure enough, she could see the crime scene team there. "I'm really over yellow police tape." It was flapping in the wind. "This is going to destroy business." When word spread that her gallery had been the scene of a murder…

Eric wrapped his arm around her shoulder. "No, you're not looking at it the right way. You'll get a ton of press. And you'll get all of the curiosity seekers who want to come by. Business will boom."

She threw him a doubting glance.

He shrugged. "Glass half full, okay? Not empty."

Piper could only shake her head. They headed for the front of the tattoo shop. There was a neon sign to the right of the store, and the green letters glowed OPEN. She entered the shop, and a little bell jingled overhead.

But no one was behind the counter.

"Mark?" Piper called.

The black curtains behind the counter parted, and he rushed out, a smile on his face. "Piper!" But the smile dimmed when he saw— "Eric?"

Mark stopped. "You...is the protection detail still going on?"

Eric's arm was around Piper's shoulders. She felt him stiffen.

"He's not here as protection." She lifted her chin. "We're together."

Mark's gaze jumped between them both. "Oh. *Oh.*" He winced. "Sorry, Eric, didn't mean any disrespect. Just thought, you know, you two were...not like that. After what Piper said the other day, you know, about you being the bodyguard and all..."

"Things have changed. We're like that," Eric said flatly.

Mark shuffled to the counter. His hands tapped against the surface. "I...shit, I haven't slept since last night. I got out of the police station when the sun was rising, and I-I just came here. But when I got here, the crime scene team was spread out all over the street. They are CSI-ing the shit out of your place, by the way, and every time I glance over there..." He flattened his hands on the counter. "*God,* I killed a man."

Piper pulled from Eric and walked toward Mark. He looked so beaten and haggard. "You need rest. You should go home." *And not just stare at the scene of the crime.*

His gaze searched hers. Dark shadows lined his eyes. "You're okay, though. You're safe. He can never hurt you. That's what matters."

"I'm safe," she agreed softly.

Behind her, Eric's phone rang. She looked back and found him frowning at the screen. "It's Layla," he told her. "Give me one second."

He headed outside, and the bell jingled over the door.

Piper glanced back at Mark. She found that he was already watching her.

"You're...really with him?" His voice was low, as if he didn't want Eric to overhear. "You sure that guy is your type?"

"I'm sure he's the guy I want." Her hand reached for Mark's and squeezed. "Mark, I know you must be going through hell. Have you contacted your sponsor?" That was the main reason she'd wanted to see him that morning. To make sure he was okay. To make sure that he didn't turn back to the bottle.

He shook his head. "I...I need to."

She nodded.

"My phone's in the back." He exhaled. "I could...I could use a friend with me. Come with me while I make the call?"

"Of course." She spared a quick glance through the window. Eric was right outside. He met her stare through the glass. She gave him a little wave.

Then Piper followed Mark through the black curtain and into the back of the shop. The walls were filled with sketches. So much artwork. So many tattoo photos. Mark was an incredible artist. She'd tried to get him to do some work so that she could put it up in her gallery and—

"I saved you."

He stood near a tattoo work station. His shoulders were bowed, and his hands were loose at his sides. She could see his phone, tossed onto the chair at the station.

"I killed him, and I saved you."

"Mark—"

His head lifted. Rage twisted his face. "So why the fuck are you still with that sonofabitch Eric? *You should be with me.*"

***

"Layla, I can't make out everything you're saying. Our connection is shit." Eric peered through the glass. Where had Piper gone? "You're fading in and out on me."

"The sister had eleven stab wounds!"

Okay, he'd finally heard her, loud and clear. But he wasn't following—

"Mark Rogue's sister!" She was practically screaming. "Eleven—" She cut out again and came back with, *"Stab wounds!"*

Fucking hell.

"Where is Piper?" Layla blasted. "I went to Mark's home, but he wasn't there."

Now he could hear her perfectly. "He's at his shop, and so is Piper." He ran for the front of the building. Yanked open the door. The fucking bell jingled. "*Piper!*"

The thunder of a gunshot nearly stopped his heart.

***

She'd taken him down. When Mark had lunged at her, Piper had fought back. She'd punched the bastard in the face and kicked him in the left knee with all of her strength. He'd gone down, shouting at her, and he'd nearly slammed into the tattoo station.

At that point, she'd whirled for the door—
Bam!

A gunshot fired, and the bullet slammed into her shoulder. Piper staggered and nearly fell, but—

"I will shoot you again if you don't *freeze!*"

Piper froze because she knew her back was a perfect target.

The black curtains that led to the front of the shop were about five feet away, and as she watched, they flew open. Eric appeared, his face wild and his eyes burning with fury.

Piper could feel the blood sliding down her arm.

Eric's gaze went to the blood, and his eyes widened. His body stiffened as he—

"If you move, Eric, I will fire a bullet into her spine. I hit what I aim for." Mark's voice was a furious snarl. "That's why she just has a wound in her shoulder so far. But if you play hero or if she tries to get away again, I'll make sure she never runs again. Never runs. Never walks. Barely even moves at all."

"You fucking sonofabitch!" Eric shouted. She saw his hand moving toward his coat and she couldn't remember…did he have a weapon on him? Didn't he usually have a weapon of some sort? But she didn't remember seeing a gun holster on him that day.

Did he have a knife? Something else?

Her shoulder was pulsing as the blood kept dripping down her arm.

"You were supposed to turn to me, Piper," Mark snapped. "*I* saved the day. You were supposed to be grateful to me. You were supposed to come back to me. I wanted you all this time. I waited for you. I set this whole stage so that you'd see I was the protector you needed. *You were supposed to come back to me.*"

Piper was staring straight at Eric. She saw his rage and his fear and his deadly determination.

"Not him! Stop focusing on him!" A scream from Mark. "Face me!"

She slowly turned toward Mark. He'd staggered to his feet and he seemed to be favoring his left leg. Savagely, Piper hoped she'd freaking shattered his knee cap.

With one hand, he held on to the chair, and with the other, he gripped a gun. Mark laughed when he saw her gaze fall to his weapon. "Had it hidden at my work station. Just in case, you know. I-I don't like guns. They're too rough, too loud, but they can get the job done. I don't like them, though, I like—"

"You like knives, don't you?" Eric called out.

Mark flinched.

"You like knives…just like the one you used on your sister."

The gun trembled in Mark's grasp.

Shock rolled through Piper. His sister?

"Eleven stab wounds," Eric added fiercely. "That's a very precise number."

Was Eric closer? His voice definitely sounded closer. She hadn't heard the sound of his feet moving…*ninja skills.*

"Your sister had eleven wounds. Just like Grady Fox did."

"Shut up!" Mark yelled. Spittle flew from his mouth.

"And *you* were the one to find your sister's body." Eric's voice pounded at him. "Or at least, that's what you told the cops. You found her. But I'm thinking you were just *there* when she was attacked. Because you're the bastard who killed her!"

"Shut up!" Mark lifted the gun higher. Aimed it right at Piper's head. "And stop walking! Don't move again! Stay where you are or I will shoot her!"

She could feel Eric behind her.

"You hurt Piper," Eric said, his voice going quiet and cold. "All along, it was you."

Her breath came fast. "Why?"

"I needed you back!"

"Why did you start drinking, Mark?" Eric asked, the words even softer. "It wasn't because your sister was dead, was it? It was because you couldn't stomach what you'd done."

But Mark laughed. "No, you're so wrong. It was because I wanted to do it *again*. I liked it. I liked it when she screamed. She was always such an uppity bitch. The golden child while I was just the tattooed freak. I stopped that. I stopped *her*. And I wanted to do it again, but I couldn't. I couldn't…"

"Because then there would be a pattern," Piper said, understanding. "And you wouldn't get away with murder."

He smiled at her. "When I was with you, I didn't want to hurt anyone else. I was happy, *and* I wasn't drinking. So I thought, if we could just be together again, everything would be fine."

Piper shook her head. "Nothing is fine. You killed Grady. And…Jessica?"

A bored shrug. "I fucked her. I mean, I wasn't fucking you — you with all of your no touch rules. But Jessica liked to get dirty, and she liked it often. I fucked her until she fell for that dumbass Dante. Then I think she started to get suspicious because she was asking me questions so…" A shrug. "I made her go away."

Nausea rose in her.

"I like the knife. If the ME looks at Jessica close enough, he'll see Jessica had wounds before she died." A shrug. "If anyone bothers to look that close. I found that people don't, not usually. They see what they want to see."

Like…with Dante. They'd seen a killer who'd been stopped. They hadn't seen a victim.

"Why was Dante in my gallery?" Piper asked, trying to keep the guy talking.

A smirk. "Because that's where I put him. Grady wasn't the only one I lured to town, though I didn't use your email for Dante. He was so fucking clueless. I kept him tied up at my house, and he spilled all kinds of shit. He had paintings of you and Jessica. Said they were art. Said he was just an artist looking for beauty. Screw that. When I heard about the paintings, I knew he could be the fall guy. I could tie everything up, all nice and neat, and then I could have you." Fury flashed in his eyes. *"But you're fucking this bastard! You're messing everything up!* It was supposed to just be a lie — Eric said you were with him, but you weren't. He was your bodyguard, nothing else, it wasn't supposed to be —"

"How did Dante get the stab wound to his chest?" Eric demanded. He was right behind Piper. She could feel him. Strong and solid. And…

His fingers slid down her arm. Squeezed.

"I gave him that wound," Mark boasted. "Had to match up after Ben's jerkoff self told the cops he'd stabbed his attacker." A rough laugh. "He *tried* to stab me, but I was wearing my Kevlar vest. All he did was bruise me, but I hid that with a new tat." The gun finally left her as he jerked open the coat he was wearing to reveal a bulky, black vest covering his torso. "Put it on when I got back here this morning. Bought the damn thing at the department store—a freaking work vest made with Kevlar. Ninety bucks. Had no idea it would be a game changer for me."

The gun still wasn't pointing at her because he was gesturing to his vest and—

Eric grabbed her. He shoved Piper behind him and stepped forward. Mark yelled and brought up his gun, screaming, but Eric was already attacking. Eric had yanked out a knife— *he'd definitely been packing a weapon* – and he threw it toward Mark. The blade hurtled end over end and lodged into Mark's neck.

The bullet went wild. She heard it thud into the wall.

Eric leapt forward and so did Piper. She kicked the gun out of Mark's grasp even as he sank to his knees. His eyes were open and terrified, and he immediately grabbed for the knife.

"Don't pull it out!" Eric yelled.

Too late. Mark yanked the knife out, and blood *poured* from the wound.

Mark fell back. His fingers were soaked with blood. His legs were twitching and jerking. His hands flopped to his sides. The knife clattered to the floor.

"Shit!" Eric shoved his hands over Mark's throat.

They needed an ambulance or the guy was going to die. Piper knew it. And maybe — dammit, maybe it would be better if he died. After what he'd done to Grady and Jessica. To his own sister…

*But…*God, could she watch a man die? Piper grabbed the gun and whirled to find a phone. *There.* She saw one on a nearby counter. She dialed frantically and demanded the ambulance. When she whirled back around, her gaze locked on the nightmare scene.

Eric was trying to save Mark. And Mark — he'd just picked up the knife. His blood-covered fingers curled around the handle. He was about to drive it into Eric's side even as Eric fought to keep the bastard alive.

"Eric, get back!" Piper screamed.

Without hesitation, he lunged back.

"Drop it, Mark!" Piper aimed the gun at him. No one was going to hurt Eric. No one.

Mark smiled. Surged up at her —

She fired. One bullet. One fast thunder. One hit right in the middle of his head.

One hit.

One terrible, horrifying hit. *Oh, God. The blood.*

Silence.

The bell over the front door jingled, and Piper jerked. Footsteps rushed toward them and the black curtain flew open. She aimed her gun straight at—Layla Lopez. The gun trembled in her hands. *I shot him in the head. Had to—he was wearing the vest. I didn't know if the bullet could go through the vest. I shot him in the head and the blood flew out and—*

Layla licked her lips. "You know I need you to drop that weapon."

Her teeth were chattering. "I-I need to make sure he's not going to attack again."

"He's gone," Eric told her quietly.

Her head whipped toward him. He was beside Mark's body, his fingers at Mark's throat.

"He's gone, baby. You can put the gun down."

Gone.

The gun felt too heavy in her hand, but she lowered it slowly, oddly terrified that if she just dropped it, the gun would go off. The bullet would fly out and someone would get hurt again.

A shudder rippled over Piper's body. "I killed him."

"I swear, I did this scene already." Layla blew out a hard breath. Then she strode toward Mark. Blood-covered Mark. "Told you, sonofabitch, I don't stop until I catch the killer. Knew it was you, as soon as I read your sister's case file. Couldn't leave the office, not until I did it."

Eric moved to stand in front of Piper. "Baby?"

He was okay. She threw her arms around him and held tight. As tight as she could. Piper never, ever intended to let him go.

In that one moment, that one terrible moment when Mark had lunged up with the knife, she'd known that she would do anything to protect Eric. She'd squeezed the trigger fully aware that she was killing so that he wouldn't be hurt.

She loved Eric. And if anyone threatened the man she loved again...

I will always defend him.

"Baby, I think I almost had a heart attack." He wasn't holding her back. He was stiff within her embrace. "And all I want to do is put my arms around you, but I've got his blood all over my hands. I love you so much. So freaking much and I *never, ever* want to find some bastard holding a gun on you again and—*Shit! She's shot!*"

And Piper became aware of the burn in her shoulder. A burn that she'd been ignoring until that moment.

As she pulled back from Eric, she saw that her whole left sleeve was soaked with blood. And her shoulder...damn, was the bullet still inside of her? Her head turned as she craned to see the wound.

It pulsed blood. Heavy rivers that poured every few moments. And the blood wasn't just *dripping* down her arm.

It was more like *pouring* down her arm.

A siren screamed in the distance.

She felt her knees start to buckle. No way. She was not passing out after everything that had just happened. She locked her knees, but that only made the sudden light-headedness worse.

"I've got you." Eric was there. "You protected me, and *I've got you.*"

Nice words. Wonderful words. But it was more like… "We have each other," she whispered.

He smiled at her.

She didn't pass out. Did. Not.

The ambulance's scream grew louder.

"I need a new tattoo…" Piper whispered. "Can't let his mark stay on me. I won't. Gonna have to get that moon changed into something else."

EPILOGUE

"Okay, you're going to be pissed, but you need help."

Piper glanced up, frowning when she saw Ben's reflection in the mirror. He looked all suave and debonair in his tux, his hair perfectly in place while she—

God, she felt like a hot mess.

"Isn't your maid of honor supposed to help you with pre-wedding rituals?" Ben asked pointedly. Then he frowned over at the maid in question.

Layla glanced up from the magazine she'd been reading. The Rock smiled from the cover. Layla lifted a brow at Ben. "Getting dressed isn't a ritual. I think Piper can handle that all on her own."

"No, forget getting dressed. She's dressed. The gown is on. She's got the flowers. I was talking about the *other* stuff." He wiggled his brows. "The something old, the something new, the—"

"The something borrowed, something blue," Layla finished. Sighing, she put down Dwayne

Johnson. "I am a detective. I have taken care of these things. Her dress is new, her underwear is old—"

"OhmyGod." Piper squeezed her eyes closed. "You two are such trouble when you get together."

"I let her *borrow* my necklace. Thank you very much." Layla glanced at her nails. "Really, all she needs is—"

"Something blue," Ben announced flatly. "And if she doesn't have it, she's going to start her marriage with bad luck. Can't we all agree that we've had enough of that?"

Piper rolled back her shoulders. "I don't think Mark counts as bad luck." She rolled back her shoulders again. Just for fun. The dress was strapless, and she liked the way the soft satin felt when she did the little roll.

"He counts more as a psychotic," Layla agreed, "if you ask me."

Ben's face peered next to Piper's in the mirror. "I see no blue. Not even a hint. Not anywhere."

"Your eyes are blue," she told him. "And you're usually in my space. Doesn't that count?"

He smiled. Dimples flashed. "It does if I get to be the one walking you down the aisle."

Her lips parted. She didn't know what to say.

"Your asshole dad isn't here. You invited him, I know you did. Eric gave you the guy's address, and then he made sure an agent personally delivered the fellow's invitation."

She had to swallow the lump in her throat.

"Your prick of a dad didn't come, so fuck him." Ben's voice was completely flat. "You don't need him. You have a family that loves you. So…if it's okay with you…" He backed up.

She turned to face him.

Ben offered his arm to her. "It would be my honor to walk you down the aisle."

She reached for his arm. "I'm not pissed by the offer of your help." Piper leaned onto her toes and kissed his cheek. "But I am touched. Yes, Ben, I'd like that very much."

***

The music was playing. The church was full of people. But Piper wasn't walking down the aisle.

Where was she? Shouldn't she have appeared by now? Eric pulled at the collar of his shirt.

And where was his damn best man? Ben had stood beside him earlier, but now the guy had pulled a disappearing act. If the fellow ruined this wedding, Eric was going to kick his younger brother's ass.

Piper. Main issue is Piper. He couldn't relax, not until he saw her. Eric still had this terrible feeling that she was going to turn away from him, that he'd lose his dream. He couldn't take a deep enough breath, not until he saw her.

Simon slid from the front pew. "Man, you look like you're about to pass out."

Everybody stood up. Jesus. They were in his way. He strained to see around them. "My dumbass brother is missing—"

"No," Simon corrected him. "He's right where he's supposed to be."

Then Eric saw her. Saw them.

Piper was walking down the aisle. She was carrying a bouquet of blood-red roses, and when she saw Eric, a giant smile curled her beautiful lips.

She wasn't alone. Ben was at her side. They walked together as they came toward Eric.

And…

Eric understood. Understood so much.

His shoulders straightened as he hurried to meet her. There were murmurs from the crowd, but screw them. Piper was his partner. And he couldn't wait.

Ben laughed, and he inclined his head to Eric. "She'll always be my best friend." Sadness came and went in his eyes. "But she'll be so much more to you." He clapped his hand on Eric's shoulder. "Love her, cherish her, and always protect her…or I swear I will kick your ass, big brother or not."

Love her, cherish her, and always protect her. "She's my life." If he didn't keep her happy, he'd deserve that ass kicking.

Eric took Piper's hand in his. Held her carefully, oddly worried he'd crush her.

Her smile was the most beautiful thing he'd ever seen. Later, he'd tell his brother and parents that he didn't remember a single word the priest said. Eric wouldn't even remember what *he'd* said, but he would easily recall when Piper told him…

"It's okay. I think you're supposed to kiss me now."

Because then he could breathe again. A nice, deep breath.

And he kissed his bride.

The End

A NOTE FROM THE AUTHOR

Thank you so much for reading PROTECTING PIPER! This was such a fun book to write. I liked the way that Piper looked at the world—slightly off-centered. I've always enjoyed the enemies-to-lovers story-line, and when you throw in some bodyguard fun…well, this book was just an absolute pleasure to write! I hope that you enjoyed it! If you did, please consider leaving a review of the story. Reviews help new readers to discover awesome new books.

If you'd like to stay updated on my releases and sales, please join my newsletter list.

https://cynthiaeden.com/newsletter/

Best,
Cynthia Eden
cynthiaeden.com

ABOUT THE AUTHOR

Cynthia Eden is a *New York Times*, *USA Today*, *Digital Book World*, and *IndieReader* best-seller.

Cynthia writes sexy tales of contemporary romance, romantic suspense, and paranormal romance. Since she began writing full-time in 2005, Cynthia has written over one hundred novels and novellas.

Cynthia lives along the Alabama Gulf Coast. She loves romance novels, horror movies, and chocolate.

For More Information
- *https://cynthiaeden.com*
- *http://www.facebook.com/cynthiaedenfanpage*
- *http://www.twitter.com/cynthiaeden*

HER OTHER WORKS

Wilde Ways
- Protecting Piper (Wilde Ways, Book 1)
- Guarding Gwen (Wilde Ways, Book 2)
- Before Ben (Wilde Ways, Book 3)
- The Heart You Break (Wilde Ways, Book 4)
- Fighting For Her (Wilde Ways, Book 5)
- Ghost Of A Chance (Wilde Ways, Book 6)

Dark Sins
- Don't Trust A Killer (Dark Sins, Book 1)
- Don't Love A Liar (Dark Sins, Book 2)

Lazarus Rising
- Never Let Go (Book One, Lazarus Rising)
- Keep Me Close (Book Two, Lazarus Rising)
- Stay With Me (Book Three, Lazarus Rising)
- Run To Me (Book Four, Lazarus Rising)

- Lie Close To Me (Book Five, Lazarus Rising)
- Hold On Tight (Book Six, Lazarus Rising)
- Lazarus Rising Volume One (Books 1 to 3)
- Lazarus Rising Volume Two (Books 4 to 6)

Dark Obsession Series

- Watch Me (Dark Obsession, Book 1)
- Want Me (Dark Obsession, Book 2)
- Need Me (Dark Obsession, Book 3)
- Beware Of Me (Dark Obsession, Book 4)
- Only For Me (Dark Obsession, Books 1 to 4)

Mine Series

- Mine To Take (Mine, Book 1)
- Mine To Keep (Mine, Book 2)
- Mine To Hold (Mine, Book 3)
- Mine To Crave (Mine, Book 4)
- Mine To Have (Mine, Book 5)
- Mine To Protect (Mine, Book 6)
- Mine Series Box Set Volume 1 (Mine, Books 1-3)
- Mine Series Box Set Volume 2 (Mine, Books 4-6)

Bad Things

- The Devil In Disguise (Bad Things, Book 1)
- On The Prowl (Bad Things, Book 2)
- Undead Or Alive (Bad Things, Book 3)
- Broken Angel (Bad Things, Book 4)
- Heart Of Stone (Bad Things, Book 5)
- Tempted By Fate (Bad Things, Book 6)
- Bad Things Volume One (Books 1 to 3)
- Bad Things Volume Two (Books 4 to 6)
- Bad Things Deluxe Box Set (Books 1 to 6)
- Wicked And Wild (Bad Things, Book 7)
- Saint Or Sinner (Bad Things, Book 8)

Bite Series

- Forbidden Bite (Bite Book 1)
- Mating Bite (Bite Book 2)

Blood and Moonlight Series

- Bite The Dust (Blood and Moonlight, Book 1)
- Better Off Undead (Blood and Moonlight, Book 2)
- Bitter Blood (Blood and Moonlight, Book 3)
- Blood and Moonlight (The Complete Series)

Purgatory Series

- The Wolf Within (Purgatory, Book 1)

- Marked By The Vampire (Purgatory, Book 2)
- Charming The Beast (Purgatory, Book 3)
- Deal with the Devil (Purgatory, Book 4)
- The Beasts Inside (Purgatory, Books 1 to 4)

Bound Series

- Bound By Blood (Bound Book 1)
- Bound In Darkness (Bound Book 2)
- Bound In Sin (Bound Book 3)
- Bound By The Night (Bound Book 4)
- Forever Bound (Bound, Books 1 to 4)
- Bound in Death (Bound Book 5)

Other Romantic Suspense

- One Hot Holiday
- Secret Admirer
- First Taste of Darkness
- Sinful Secrets
- Until Death
- Christmas With A Spy

Made in the USA
Middletown, DE
05 March 2020